©Nao Watanuki

Toshio Satou

Illustration by
Nao Watanuki

Suppose
a Kid from the Last Dungeon
Boonies Moved to a Starter Town

Mina

A mysterious, beautiful actress. Handpicked by the director for the leading role.

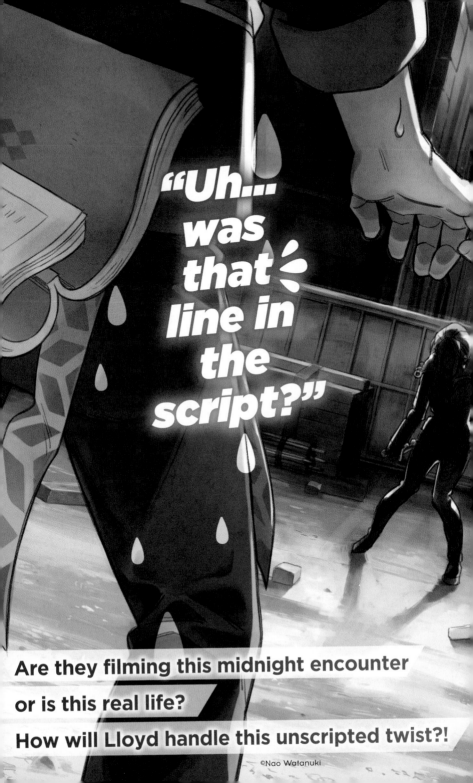

[CONTENTS]

Suppose a Kid from the Last Dungeon Boonies Moved to a Starter Town

6

Toshio Satou

Illustration by
Nao Watanuki

YEN ON
NEW YORK

Suppose a Kid from the LAST DUNGEON 6 BOONIES moved to a Starter Town

TOSHIO SATOU

Translation by Andrew Cunningham
Cover art by Nao Watanuki

TATOEBA LAST DUNGEON MAENO MURANO SHOUNEN GA JYOBAN NO MACHI DE KURASU YOUNA MONOGATARI volume 6
Copyright © 2019 Toshio Satou
Illustrations copyright © 2019 Nao Watanuki
All rights reserved.
Original Japanese edition published in 2019 by SB Creative Corp.

This English edition is published by arrangement with SB Creative Corp., Tokyo, in care of Tuttle-Mori Agency, Inc., Tokyo.

English translation © 2021 by Yen Press, LLC

Yen On
150 West 30th Street, 19th Floor
New York, NY 10001

Visit us at yenpress.com · facebook.com/yenpress · twitter.com/yenpress
yenpress.tumblr.com · instagram.com/yenpress

First Yen On Edition: July 2021

Yen On is an imprint of Yen Press, LLC.
The Yen On name and logo are trademarks of Yen Press, LLC.

The publisher is not responsible for websites (or their content) that are not owned by the publisher.

Library of Congress Cataloging-in-Publication Data
Names: Satou, Toshio, author. | Watanuki, Nao, illustrator. | Cunningham, Andrew, 1979– translator.
Title: Suppose a kid from the last dungeon boonies moved to a starter town / Toshio Satou ; illustration by Nao Watanuki ; translation by Andrew Cunningham.
Other titles: Tatoeba last dungeon maeno murano shounen ga jyoban no machi de kurasu youna. English
Description: First Yen On edition. | New York, NY : Yen ON, 2019–
Identifiers: LCCN 2019030186 | ISBN 9781975305666 (v. 1 ; trade paperback) |
    ISBN 9781975306236 (v. 2 ; trade paperback) | ISBN 9781975313043 (v. 3 ; trade paperback) |
    ISBN 9781975313296 (v. 4 ; trade paperback) | ISBN 9781975313319 (v. 5 ; trade paperback) |
    ISBN 9781975313333 (v. 6 ; trade paperback)
Subjects: CYAC: Adventure and adventurers—Fiction. | Self-esteem—Fiction.
Classification: LCC PZ7.1.S266 Tat 2019 | DDC [Fic]—dc23
LC record available at https://lccn.loc.gov/2019030186

ISBNs: 978-1-9753-1333-3 (paperback)
       978-1-9753-1334-0 (ebook)

10 9 8 7 6 5 4 3 2 1

LSC-C

Printed in the United States of America

Alka

Chief of the town of legend. Dotes on Lloyd like he's her own son. Casts a special spell on Lloyd so he can get some screen time.

Lloyd Belladonna

Excessively strong villager raised in the town of legend. Has come to Rokujou to be an extra in a movie!

Marie the Witch

Disguises herself as an information broker on the East Side but is actually the princess of the Azami Kingdom. Enjoys living with Lloyd too much to drop the pretense that she's a witch.

©Nao Watanuki

Allan Lidocaine

Son of a decorated noble family. Meeting Lloyd has only spread his fame.

Riho Flavin

Skilled mercenary. In it for the money. Lately seems preoccupied with Lloyd's every move.

Selen Hemein

Former Cursed Belt Princess. Devoted to Lloyd, who changed her destiny. ♥

Amidine Oxo

A bona fide movie star, famous for *Rokujou Holiday*. He's actually...?

Sardin Valyl-Tyrosine

King of Rokujou aka Dumb Dandy. Attempting to create a booming film industry.

Phyllo Quinone

A martial artist in love with Lloyd. Once lived in Rokujou with her sister, Mena.

Ubi

Assassin for the mob. Dwells in the darkness of Rokujou, struggling where light does not shine.

Mina

A beautiful actress with an air of mystery. Sardin himself plucked her out of obscurity to play the lead role.

Micona Zol

A year above Lloyd. Head over heels for Marie. Cast for the waitress role.

Chapter 1

An Inspiring Saga: Suppose a Kid from the Boonies Yearned to Be a Star

In the palace archive at the heart of Azami's Central District sat a young girl in the window frame, gazing into the distance.

She wore a white robe and was kicking her little feet, making her pigtails swing.

The room was so high up you could see the whole city, but a fall would surely prove fatal. Any other child would be quickly pulled off the sill and scolded, but this one required no such care.

Her name was Alka. She was the chief of the village at the end of the world, Kunlun. She looked to be around nine years old but was well over a hundred, and she was so powerful, she could defeat a dragon with her pinkie.

Recent events had made her power unstable and difficult to control, but she remained a superpowered kid grandma. Easily one of the most powerful people in the world. So dangerous that if you attempted to scold her, she might scold you back—and turn you to ash. Be very careful around her.

Currently, she was making the shape of a telescope with her hands and staring at the northern half of the kingdom.

The North Side was the gateway to Azami, lined with hotels and expensive restaurants, weapon and armor shops, and all manner of entertainment—a real tourist trap.

Alka's eyes were locked on one boy, observing him and his companions.

This boy was the apple of Alka's eye, Lloyd Belladonna. He came from the same village and was now a cadet in the Azami military, as were the girls with him.

"Mwa-ha-ha."

Observing might be too generous. *Peeping* was more like it… She was a weird one.

"Master, what are you doing?"

The speaker wore a pointy black hat and a robe of the same color festooned with elaborate decorative touches. Clearly, she was a witch. Her name was Marie, and she was busy tapping the dust off a book.

"Mm? Making sure Lloyd is safe and savoring every inch of his body, obviously. Like a lifeguard at the pool! Ready to give mouth-to-mouth the moment the need arises."

A public apology to all lifeguards on her behalf: Please don't take anything a kid grandma says seriously. She's drowning in the seas of love, sinking rapidly into those murky depths. Just let her be.

"Not what lifeguards do! You make him run an errand for you and— *Bweh-choo!*"

The dust on the book made Marie sneeze violently mid-reprimand… largely undermining her point.

Alka looked at Marie the way you would a sad old man.

"Who sneezes like *that*?! You're a princess! Go for an elegant little *pssht*."

"Royalty sneeze like everyone else! And whose fault is it I'm— *Bwah-choo!*"

Marie's real name was Maria Azami, the actual princess of this entire kingdom. Currently, she lived on the East Side, calling herself Marie the Witch.

The reasons for this were long and complicated. She'd been avoiding governmental tensions, fleeing the threat of a political marriage… The latter wouldn't remain a threat if anyone saw how much snot she had on her face now.

©Nao Watanuki

Alka ignored her completely, too busy feasting her eyes on the boy below.

"Ah, my Lloyd is always adorable! But what is he looking at? Marie, what's that building?" Alka pointed at one of the newer structures.

"Oh, that's the new motion picture palace they just built."

"Motion pictures?"

"Yeah. They also call them movies? It's a brand-new form of entertainment they invented out in Rokujou. Apparently, if you show a bunch of photographs in a row, it looks like they're moving. They made this one called *Rokujou Holiday*, and the star of it, Amidine Oxo, is suddenly world-famous—"

As Marie gushed, Alka started to frown.

"Movies? At this level of technology? Dr. Eug's gotta be behind it."

Dr. Eug. Like Alka, she was immortal. Her goal was to increase the technological sophistication of this fantasy world, creating a hybrid of magic and science.

…That sounded like a good thing, but the way she was going about it was all wrong.

Specifically, she planned to use the demon lords to place the world in peril, making mankind desperate enough to accept weapons and technology that were entirely out of place in this fantasy setting. A drowning man will clutch at straws, so if a nuclear-powered submarine passed by… Well, that was Eug's argument anyway.

Her last plans had been squashed by others, but she'd fled to the Jiou Empire—which was already under the control of her allies—and had clearly already nocked a second arrow.

She was thorough, to say the least.

"I guess this was an insurance policy in case her last plan didn't work?" Alka sighed. "So she had her fingers in Rokujou, too…"

Certainly, people tended to accept unknown technology and devices if they promised to be entertaining. Like learning how to operate a computer so you can play an adult game. Look, it's just an example!

"She's using entertainment to force society to progress and place herself in control of the world's economies… That would take a long time, though. We've gotta assume she's still trying to free the demon lords."

"Uh, Master? What's up?" Marie asked.

"Oh," Alka said, emerging from her thoughts. "Sorry, sorry. You found what we're looking for?"

Marie finished wiping her snot with a handkerchief and handed over the book, looking exhausted.

"Will this do?" she asked. "This is something you could never look at without my permission, so you could be a little grateful."

"Thanks, thanks. If you die, I'll light you a candle—no, three!"

"Planning on outliving me? …Geez."

Alka snatched the book and started flipping through it.

The title on the cover was *Fantastic Beasts and Treasure in Azami*.

This was a compendium of investigations and reports on monster sightings and damages, as well as legendary equipment (known as *artifacts*) and cursed items. It wasn't just verified data, but rumors, too.

You might wonder what was so special about it. National records were extremely detailed and not something just anyone could look at. For example, this report had a chart of a jewelry shop's security cameras and safety measures, as well as data on their business rivals. This was a set of documents that would make poachers and enemy governments froth at the mouth.

Alka was whipping through the book so fast, it was hard to believe she was reading any of it.

"Hmm, I see, I see."

"So why did you want to see this book anyway?"

"I'm looking for a beast that can replace Vritra as Kunlun's guardian. With my powers in flux, life has been a pain. Was hoping there'd be some handy-dandy monster or demon lord out there that conveniently understood human words."

"Huh…" Marie looked slightly stunned. *Handy-dandy* wasn't often used as a descriptor for a demon lord. Especially delivered in the sort of tone an understaffed convenience store owner might use when hoping they'd find someone with a good personality willing to work the night shift.

"But Azami just has small fries… How peaceful! Rokujou's got a few rare monsters… The Ascorbic Domain, huh? Gotta check these artifacts, too. Lots of those will hint at a demon lord's location or might outright transform into one of those beasts."

"Uh, really? I mean, I guess Selen's cursed belt did turn out to be Vritra's hide…"

"The cursed belt… Oh, that's in here, too. Man, all I did was accidentally mix my apron in with the pasta dough, so seeing it get an article like this—it makes a lady blush."

"You don't even look remotely guilty… Wait, this one looks like it could be a clue to pin down a demon lord." Marie pointed at a sketch of a basic-looking pendant.

"Oh! That's the Saint's Pendant. I remember that! This claims it can banish evil spirits."

"You're familiar with it?"

"Yep. I made it. Also, the banishing evil part is a load of hooey. If you spin the thing around, it'll make a tornado and blow evil spirits away along with the person holding it, shop signs, houses, cows, sharks, you name it!"

Like a hurricane in a Hollywood movie.

"…What about that says 'Saint'?"

This seemed a reasonable point, but Alka just looked proud.

"Well, I made it! And I'm a saint. Mwa-ha-ha-ha-ha!"

Why make something like that at all? Marie thought, but she decided it would be better to discuss a different artifact instead.

"What about this jewel…? Did you make it, too?"

The page called it the Jewel of Legions, and it was apparently red like blood.

"'Course not! What do you think I am, some sort of dwarf?"

"Whew."

"That was made by the king of the dwarves…Eug. Uses the power of necromancy to let you stick evil spirits in anything, animate or inanimate! You can use it to summon the dead, create a zombie army… Greatest thing since sliced bread, she said."

Since when could zombies be compared to bread?

"How hard is it to slice your own bread? No, never mind that—why would she make something that terrifying in the first place?"

"Don't ask me! …Hmm… It doesn't seem like you've got any artifacts to write home about. Even with my powers destabilized, I can still whip up a tornado or two with one hand tied behind my back."

"You're more demon lordish than most demon lords."

"I agree! …Oh, this monster might make a decent guardian! It seems appropriately demon lordish."

Alka held up a page. Marie didn't really have a clue what qualified a monster for guardian status, so she glanced at it without much enthusiasm…

And the dust on the page made her sneeze again.

"Bwah-kah-choooooooooooooooo!"

"Hey! The data! All that valuable intel buried in royal jelly!"

"I'm a princess, not a bee! And stop waving that dusty thing a— *Chooo!*"

"Augh! Royal jelly in my eeeeeyes!"

Marie's spray had scored a direct hit. Alka fell over, clutching her eyes.

"Sorry…aughh! The documents!"

Fantastic Beasts and Treasure in Azami had gone flying out of Alka's hand, out the window…and landed with a splash in the pond below.

"That's really valuable, you know! What will I say if it's gone for good?!"

"Well, whose fault is it?! Go fetch!"

"Go fetch? Do you know how many floors up we— Aughhhhhh!"

"Dive! Keep trying till you find it!"

Shoved out the window into the pond below, Marie ended up getting dunked, like a fisher's trained cormorant.

The pages were soaked through and unreadable until they dried…so Kunlun would have to do without a guardian for a while longer.

A few hours after Marie's successful cormoranting…

At Reiyoukaku, the luxury hotel near the Rokujou-Azami border… world leaders huddled in a room designed for successful merchants and government officials, concerned looks on every face.

The sign outside the room read COUNTERMEASURE CONFERENCE AGAINST THE JIOU EMPIRE, beautifully written by the hotel's calligrapher.

Jiou was threatening war with Azami, backed by the power of the demon lords. Azami was now meeting with nearby heads of state to discuss what could be done.

"We have to assume they have total control of the Jiou Empire," one woman said forcefully. She had a cloth slung over her shoulders kimono-style and a blade decorated with woven thread cradled in her arms.

This was the ruler of the Ascorbic Domain, Anzu Kyounin. She was a powerful figure who had worked her way to this position at quite a young age and seemed ready to accept a duel at any given second. She was clearly the "everyone's big sister" type.

"Exactly. The Jiou Empire declared war and unleashed demon lord minions in Azami. I was there. It was unnerving, to say the least."

Across from Anzu was the representative of the local lords, Threonine Toin Lidocaine. Having settled his long-standing feud with the Hemein family, he was keeping himself very busy ensuring all the local lords were on the same page. That was why he'd been invited here.

"There's a flood of refugees pouring over the Jiou border into Azami with no signs of abating. We can only surmise that they've been taken over by a demon lord or the equivalent and have ceased to function as a government."

This was the king of Azami, Luke Thistle Azami. Marie's father, he was a man of mercy and dignity. Albeit somewhat prone to trying too hard.

"This place has an outdoor bath? I can't wait to soak in those waters, staring up at the night sky."

Next to Anzu was a mysterious individual dressed in a rabbitlike mascot costume. From the voice, you could just barely tell she was female.

She—and what she'd said—was so jarringly out of place that everyone elected to ignore her.

"Yes, and the Jiou monks fled to Azami as well, huh? That's a blow to their anti-magic defenses and a sign their religious governance is in tatters, too. That makes it hard to see Jiou as much of a threat. We can strike them down in no time."

Anzu gripped her sword tightly, looking ready to charge in right now.

"All that proves is their confidence in their trump card—the power of the demon lord. Having been controlled by it myself, I know just how fearsome it can be," King Luke said, his voice tinged with regret. "We must proceed with caution."

The bunny hopped in again. "They've got a sauna? One with mist? If only they had a cold bath as well!"

"I'm sorry," Luke said. This was really disrupting the vibe. "Could you stop talking about baths?"

"You go from the sauna to the cold bath and back... Oh, sorry, I've been so busy lately, my autonomic nerves are out of whack."

"Lady Eve, this is an important meeting. Try to take it seriously."

"You got it!" She bowed apologetically...with all the overexaggeration of an amusement park mascot.

Eve Profen might have been wearing a crazy costume, but she was actually the ruler of Profen, a large country in the central region.

For generations, her family had been capable of conversing with animals and monsters, and they had used that talent to persuade or expel dangerous creatures, helping their country expand…and the costumes certainly made them memorable.

"The baths are one thing, but is that costume really necessary, Lady Eve?"

"Don't be silly, Anzy. Infrared light is hell on the skin."

Eve wore this outfit at all times. Nobody knew what she really looked like. She was an enigma to them all.

"We don't have time for this."

"Sorry, Anzy. But with everything that happened during the foundation-day festival in Azami, how can I dare show my face?!"

"You're just looking for any old excuse!"

"Eh-heh-heh."

Even as she chuckled, Eve gave the king of Azami a sidelong glance through the eyes of her costume.

"Mmph…" Luke made a face. During the festival in question, he'd been under the control of the demon lord Abaddon. If things had gone differently, he might well have been a threat to everyone here.

"Well, the weight loss has done wonders for you, so we'll call it even," Eve said, somehow managing to take a sip of water. Then she launched into her own interpretation of events. "I bet it's just like with Lukester here, and the Jiou emperor is possessed. It might be better to attack at once, before he can get his pieces all lined up!"

"But with no idea what their plans are, we can't afford to be rash," Threonine argued, stroking his mustache. "We may well end up blowing valuable resources on nothing. And there are all kinds of demon lords…"

"Since when are you so chill, Threonon?"

"Lady Eve, please don't call me that."

They clearly had some history together. He spoke like he was dealing with an aunt who refused to stop babying him.

Anzu propped one elbow on the table, scowling. "So our main goal today is to get on the same page? You want to make sure we're on board with a wait-and-see approach."

"That, and to ensure we're all on alert. To make certain none of you are tempted by the false promises of these dubious individuals, we're sharing all the information we have."

Eve took the packet he handed her, returning a blown kiss. "The man of the hour! The one who pretended to be the Jiou emperor! Nobody can properly describe him, it seems. Is this some sort of spell?"

Eve and Anzu read through the information. Then Anzu voiced a different question.

"By the way, about our absent guest... Is he late? Or sick?"

"I don't think he's sick. I don't think Rokujou's Dumb Dandy is capable of getting ill."

At that exact moment, the doors to the room were flung open, and a man leaped in, striking a dramatic pose.

"Fear not! I am here!"

"""""   """""

This dumbfounding entrance earned him a series of silent glares.

Paying no heed to pity or scorn, the blond man flashed his pearly whites, maintaining his pose.

"...King Sardin."

"Mm? Yes! It is I, the world-famous King Sardin!"

King Sardin Valyl-Tyrosine.

Ruler of Rokujou...he was certainly quite a character. One of those people who's always at after-party levels of enthusiasm without the aid of any alcohol. Despite this, he was a highly effective politician. His reputation boiled down to "He'd be perfect if he wasn't so cringe," and the people and his own government tended to treat him with bemusement.

"Can I cut him?"

"Anzy, he *is* technically a king. It could start a war? I think Jiou is enough of a problem."

Sardin just laughed off both the threat and the word *technically*. He must get both a lot.

"You were pretty late!" Luke scolded. "Did something come up?"

"Glad you asked!" Sardin beamed, pointing dramatically. He bent backward *really* far. "I'm late because I was fretting over the perfect pose! You must forgive me! Here, I have signed photos for everyone!"

Sardin dug these out of his pocket like business cards, but they were all photos of him striking stupid poses.

"Can I cut him *and* these photos?" Anzu asked, scowling at a photo of him shirtless.

"Anzy, make sure you do that when no one's looking. We *would* have to try and stop you."

…So she was totally fine with the actual death.

Once Sardin had given everyone a photograph, he flashed an even broader smile and threw out a thumbs-up.

"Ha-ha-ha! I jest, of course! There were many reasons! To name one, Rokujou is all about movies now! As the king, as the great Sardin, I have so much to do!"

"Hmm, those are quite popular in Azami as well," Luke noted. "*Rokujou Holiday* did boffo box office."

Sardin looked pleased to hear it. "Delightful! But this meeting is about Jiou, yes? Your basic 'don't make any careless moves and make sure we all stay in touch' deal?"

The way he jumped straight to the point without breaking his smile made Anzu clutch her head. "That's what I hate most about you," she growled.

"You always were perceptive," Threonine said.

Sardin looked bashful but failed to drop his pose.

"Oh, anyone would assume as much! So don't you go attacking Jiou willy-nilly, Anzu! They might well do a number on you! We must all join hands and find the right moment to attack together!"

"I don't need anyone holding my hand! Do a number on me, will they? Bring it. I'm ready to show the Ascorbic Domain's true power anytime!"

"Mm? By the way…," Sardin said, "when's dinner? I've heard the food here is amazing!"

This seemed to infuriate Anzu even further, but they were interrupted by a soft voice. "Pardon me. Your meals are ready."

This voice belonged a boy who clearly hadn't grown into his uniform. He was pushing a cart of food, accompanied by the powerfully bald proprietor.

"Oh, was my late arrival delaying dinner? Let's dig in!"

Sardin straightened his collar, tucked a napkin down his shirtfront, and was about to dive in…when there was a loud crash.

Anzu's chair had fallen over. She was on her guard, hand on the hilt of her sword, looking ready to fight to the death.

"Hmm…" Next to her, Eve folded her arms, appraising the boy.

"What…? What's going on?"

"It's just the food, Anzu. What's gotten into you?" Sardin asked.

Anzu ignored him, eyes trained on the boy, hackles raised.

Threonine waved her down. "Don't worry, Anzu. He's not your enemy."

"You're sure, Threonine? But…he's incredibly strong…"

The proprietor winced, bowing his head. "I apologize for the late introduction," he said. "My name is Coba Lamin, owner of this hotel. And this boy…"

Coba patted the kid on the back. The boy looked surprised, but he soon managed a gentle smile and bowed.

"Oh, right! I'm Lloyd Belladonna. I work part-time here, somedim—times."

The boy tripped over his words a bit, and Anzu finally relaxed.

"Part-time? With that much strength radiating off him?"

"Anzy, you're all in a lather! I know, I know. But do try and settle down."

Even Eve sounded a bit tense.

Lloyd just looked perplexed. Anzu kept her eyes glued to his every

©Nao Watanuki

move. This boy had unfathomable power…that didn't seem to match his attitude.

"Are my instincts haywire? …I should test him."

She pulled out a *kodachi*—a sword the size of her palm—and hid it beneath the table.

"Anzy!" Eve growled. Not a voice you expected from a fluffy bunny costume.

"Sorry, Eve," Anzu said. She waited for Lloyd to approach.

"Thanks for waiting, everyone," Lloyd announced. "Today, we have egg and fresh vegetable sandwiches!"

As he attempted to serve Anzu…she whipped the blade out, swinging it right at his forehead!

Just before it hit—*clang! Rattle-rattle.*

It went spinning across the floor, making an oddly comical noise.

"Mm?" Lloyd rubbed his uninjured forehead, wondering what had hit him.

"…Urp?" Anzu let out a strangled squeak.

Lloyd finished serving her.

"And this is a flavored coffee roasted with nuts."

He was acting like a fly had bonked him on his head.

"No, no, no! Stop! Wait!" Anzy screeched.

Threonine and Coba both made faces like *We used to react in the same way.*

"I sympathize. Right, Coba?"

"Entirely, Threonine."

They sure were friendly now. Both of them had seen up close what Lloyd could do.

Lloyd just looked flummoxed. "Er, is something wrong?"

"You bet there is! Explain yourself!"

"Um, Anzy? Settle down, please! You really need to choose your words wisely here!"

But, well, she'd thrown a knife at his head, and he was acting like nothing had happened, so this *was* her settled-down state.

Meanwhile, Lloyd was looking around, trying to figure out what was going on.

Then he spotted the blade on the floor. "Oh!" he exclaimed. "You dropped your silverware? Sorry, I should have noticed sooner!"

Lloyd bowed and then scooped up the knife.

"Silver...ware?"

"D-don't worry! It's our job to pick up any dropped utensils! Knives and forks! Right, Boss?"

"Mm, right you are, Lloyd." Coba beamed like a proud uncle.

"I'll get you a new knife right away... Huh? Did we always have knives like this?"

"That's mine...and it's not for eating. It's a *kodachi*," Anzu said, shaking her head.

"Oh!" Lloyd said, as if that explained it. "Sorry! I didn't realize you brought your own knife! I'll wipe it off for you, then!"

"It's not a knife... Huh?"

Lloyd had pulled out a handkerchief with some sort of symbol stitched into it.

"...Are those ancient runes?!" Eve yelped.

"Sure takes you back, right, Coba?"

"That it does, Threonine."

They sure were friendly now. (Reprise.)

Ancient runes—wisdom of yore. Well, Alka and Eug had invented them. Anyway, one of these was the *disenchant* rune, which Lloyd was currently using to wipe down Anzu's sword.

"Here you go! Clean as a whistle!"

When he handed it back, it was so polished, she could see her face in it. She looked *very* tense.

"Like a master blacksmith...but it only took a second..."

Eve seemed to have frozen to the spot, too, like a stuffed animal.

"The *disenchant* rune... He just used it like it was nothing..."

"What's gotten into you?" King Luke asked, smiling. "This boy is a cadet from Azami! I hear he helps out at this hotel in his off hours."

"He's…a soldier in Azami?" Anzu's eyes never left Lloyd.

"Oh?" Sardin smirked. "Is this boy your type, Anzu?"

"Can't you tell, King Sardin? …I suppose not. Some things can only be sensed after many battlefields." Then she turned to King Luke, her eyes sparkling like an eager child's. "Ruler of Azami! Can I have him?"

"Anzy, that's pushing it."

"Polishes blades like a master blacksmith? Possesses super strength? The Kyounin clan would love to have him!"

Slightly taken aback by Anzu's forceful negotiation tactics, King Luke politely declined.

"I may be king, but the fate of any one citizen is not mine to decide. You'll have to ask him."

An extremely rational point of view. Rather than calming down, however, Anzu immediately wheeled around to face Lloyd, grabbing his hand with all the enthusiasm of a college club recruiter at the beginning of the school year.

"Lloyd, was it? Come to my country!"

"Er…I can't. I'm sorry. I'm still in school."

Anzu looked momentarily disappointed, but she instantly recovered, taking a firm grip on his shoulders.

"Then as soon as you graduate! Or sooner—any time you fancy a vacation! I'll show you how great the Ascorbic Domain is! You'll never want to leave!"

"She's entirely forgotten that she rules the place…," Threonine said, shaking his head.

"Well, that's what's good about her!" Sardin cried helpfully. "I sometimes forget, myself. Am I primarily the king or the kingdom's greatest idol?"

Not very helpful, really. Always remember what your real job is, kids.

"Aha…so the reason you aren't in a rush to deal with Jiou is because you have human capital like him?" Eve said, getting things back on track.

Luke nodded to Threonine, who gave Sardin a copy of the documents.

"Certainly, Your Majesty," Threonine said. "King Sardin, this is the information we have on the people behind this incident..."

He soon had Sardin up to speed.

"...So be careful of anyone with no clear description."

"I will be." Sardin nodded gravely, still posing.

As their meal concluded, Eve cried out. "So the meeting's a wrap? Then it's finally bath time!"

She pulled out a bucket and a hand towel, dancing.

"Eve," Anzu said. "They won't let you in dressed like that."

"Come on, Anzy! I'll wash your back!"

"Take off the costume first! Don't rush me! Well, boys, if any demon lords mess with you, I'll be there to cut 'em down!"

Eve pushed Anzu through the door, headed for the outdoor bath.

"Yeesh." Threonine brushed his mustache. "She may rule the Ascorbic Domain, but Anzu is still very young. Hopefully, Lady Eve of the Profen Kingdom will be a good teacher to her..."

"I believe she taught you, Threonine?"

"Yes, primarily in matters of trade... Back then, it was a cat suit. Now, if only she could fix your habit of arriving late, Sardin."

Sardin just laughed off this bit of snark. "Mwa-ha-ha! I had a lot on my plate. That reminds me, King Azami..."

"Yes?"

"Jiou must have the citizens worried. Thus, I have a proposition."

"...I'm all ears."

"You see, my country is making a certain movie."

"It is?"

"And the director is yours truly, Sardin Valyl-Tyrosine! With my world-class talents, we're going to make an action spectacle: a tale of Rokujou soldiers crushing foul villains!"

"You're...personally directing this? Um..." Luke seemed unsure where this was going.

Sardin suddenly leaned in close, whispering in his ear.

"Naturally, it *is* a pet project, but it will also sell the populace on the idea that our country is strong, and they are safe. Effective propaganda! And that's where my proposition comes in."

Sardin whipped out a proposal and handed it to Luke.

"And this is?"

"The plans for the film in question. Rather than have this be exclusively Rokujou's production, I thought we could ask for assistance from Azami! We can put you in the closing credits and give you a special thanks!"

"Hmm," Threonine said. "Demonstrating the bonds between our two countries, providing further solace to the people? With Jiou causing mounting tensions everywhere, that could be highly effective."

Sardin was instantly all over him, warmly shaking his hand. "Exactly!" he boomed. "And with the focus on action, I'm looking for physically capable specimens. Sounds like Azami has a ready supply! Fine soldiers who would look great on film! Perhaps your son, Threonine?"

"Allan? Well, erm…he's not much of an actor…"

"No matter! We know how to work around that. If he can handle the stunts, we'll take care of the rest! No need to worry about the budget. Instead, we only ask that you promote the hell out of it! Here, have a photo of me—this is a secret bonus shot, not one of the six official releases! Are you in, or are you in?"

Sardin forcibly shoved a photo into King Luke's pocket, but the ruler of Azami took the offer in stride.

"We'll be happy to consider your proposal," he replied.

Sardin whistled. A secretary appeared behind him.

"Your Majesty, the time…"

"Consider it well, King Azami," Sardin said, looking momentarily serious. Then his good cheer returned. "Now, I must bid you adieu! Should you have trouble sleeping, just pretend that photo is me and hold me tight!"

Left in the wake of his storm, Luke and Threonine found the meeting room suddenly very quiet.

"Whew, quite a cast of characters, Your Majesty. Sardin was even more of a Dumb Dandy than his reputation suggests."

Threonine glared down at the photo he'd received: NO. 5: SARDIN, HOTTER THAN THE SUN. Luke, meanwhile, was smiling warmly at his photo.

"He wasn't always like that."

"You've known him a long time?"

"Yes. He was a bright boy. Maria loved him when she was little. He only turned into *this* once his father passed."

"I wonder what happened… Oh? Your Majesty?"

Threonine pointed at the photo Sardin had slipped into Luke's pocket—SECRET: SARDIN'S BACK SPEAKS VOLUMES.

Oh? Was that a message scrawled in the margin? What did it say?

Luke examined it carefully.

"……Quite a secret," he muttered.

He handed it to Threonine.

"—! This is dire news, indeed."

"It seems Rokujou is already in Jiou's hands."

King Sardin had left a note on the photo describing Rokujou's plight, begging for Azami's assistance. It said that Rokujou had been taken over by sinister forces and requested that Azami send in powerful soldiers—disguised as extras for his new film.

"If he's resorting to this…he must be under heavy scrutiny," Threonine said.

Luke nodded gravely. "Let's send him our finest soldiers and cadets. I do not wish to see anyone else suffer under the demon lords the way I did."

"We'll do everything we can, Your Majesty."

They exchanged solemn nods.

A few days later, during a break between lectures at the Azami Military Academy…

While the room was filled with the hum of student chatter, one girl was quietly reading a book.

Beautiful blond hair, cute features…and a sinister belt at her hips. Frankly, the expression on her face was far more sinister than the belt. This was the Cursed Belt Princess, Selen Hemein.

"Heh-heh-heh-heh-heh…"

What was she up to now? She looked like a teenage boy who just opened the sealed pages at the center of a dirty magazine.

"What are you reading, Selen?" the girl behind her asked.

Black hair loosely bound at the back, narrow, beady eyes, and a mithril arm as bulky as her frame wasn't. A former mercenary named Riho Flavin. She leaned forward, peering over Selen's shoulder at the book-like thing in her hands.

"Oh, Riho! This is the pamphlet from that movie we all saw together."

Selen held it up, showing her the cover: a photo of a young couple backed by a town filled with stone buildings, overlayed with the words *Rokujou Holiday* in a dramatic font.

"Yeah, you really liked that one…" Riho sounded less enthused.

"It was fabulous!" Selen cried, leaping to her feet. "Its reputation thoroughly deserved! A man and a woman of different backgrounds spending precious moments together, well aware it was not meant to last… Oh, if only I was on a date like that with the man I love!"

"So just looking at the pamphlet sends you off into a fantasy world, huh? I guess that's kinda cute."

It was almost a normal teenage girl thing to do.

"…Mm." A tall, expressionless girl tugged at Riho's sleeve.

"Huh? What's up, Phyllo?"

This was Phyllo Quinone. Physically speaking, she was almost as capable as Lloyd, but she spoke little and emoted less.

"…Mm."

"Yeah, that doesn't clear it up. I can't decode your mumbles like your sister does."

"......There." Phyllo pointed at the pamphlet. One of the actors' faces had been pasted over with a photo of Lloyd. The boy's gentle smile hovered awkwardly over a suave, elegant suit. They didn't match at all, like some sort of creepy collage.

"Ugh... Ugh!" Riho had glanced toward the actress, and yup, her face was replaced with Selen's.

Neither head matched the proportions of the body it was pasted onto, and every image of the male lead used the exact same picture of Lloyd, so the resulting pamphlet was a horrifying sight indeed.

"...No way she got permission to take his photo."

"Yeah, no."

Fantasies inspired by this nightmare pamphlet were definitely more Selen's style.

Heedless of Riho and Phyllo's qualms, Selen let out a blissful sigh.

"Art enriches the mind... Even Allan does good deeds occasionally."

"What do you mean? I do good deeds all the time!"

Hearing his name, a big man came over to them.

He had the face of a fighter and a big ax at his hip. The son of a big-shot local lord, his name was Allan Toin Lidocaine.

Allan wasn't exactly a wimp, but he was definitely the hard-luck type: One misunderstanding had somehow led to him being labeled the dragon slayer. Now people believed he could snap his fingers and summon the heroes of yore, which meant he had Azami's most power-ful military force under his command—in their minds.

In other words, this poor man was at the mercy of the rumor mill, but that did come with a few perks...like the free movie tickets they'd all used.

"...Can we get a free meal at a luxury restaurant next, please?" Phyllo requested.

"It's not that easy! Stop rubbing your hands together."

"Then fork over all your valuables, and I'll eat off the proceeds," Riho said.

"Is this a shakedown?!"

Possibly extortion.

As they teased Allan, Lloyd arrived. He'd been helping carry teaching materials. What a good boy. He put the pile on the podium and joined the group.

"What are we talking about?" he asked.

"Ah! Sir Lloyd!" Selen cried. "Allan's going to get us all a free meal at the finest restaurant on the North Side."

"Hey! Don't feed him your lies!" Allan attempted to bodily block the flow of misinformation. Riho ignored him entirely, acting like the free meal was a given.

"We'll set the date later," she said, waving a hand. "Mostly we were talking about how good that movie was."

At this, Lloyd's cheeks flushed instantly. "It *was* good!" he agreed, smiling. "I'd never seen a movie before! The acting was amazing, but the…composition, was it? You can see their faces up close or a view of the whole town. But they make it so you can pick out movements even in the distance, and oh, it was so exciting!"

Lloyd clearly ran out of words to describe it. The girls all smiled fondly at him, like he was an excited child.

"…More free tickets, please."

"*Hngg*, if Lloyd enjoys it that much, I'll certainly be on the lookout. A student must aim to please their master."

Lloyd had once rescued Allan, who had called him master ever since. Lloyd seemed to think this involved cooking instruction, however.

"Sorry I had to leave so quick afterward," Lloyd apologized. "I'd have loved to bask in the afterglow with everyone…"

"No prob," Riho said. "But what was that about?"

"Oh, I was asked to help serve at that hotel again in the evening. The king was there! I was so nervous."

"That…same evening…huh…?"

The hotel in question was on the Rokujou border, a good half-day ride—on a very fast horse—from Azami.

"I'd been there before, so it only took an hour," Lloyd explained cheerily.

This fresh reminder of Lloyd's powers left everyone speechless.

Oblivious to that, Lloyd was talking about the movie again.

"The actors were so into their roles! Their emotions went straight to the heart!"

Phyllo nodded. "...I agree. When the actress left the castle to meet her mother, I was totally on her side."

"Wow, that's a surprise. You usually never think about anything but fighting," Riho commented.

".........I'm also searching for my mother."

"Oh?"

"...She's missing."

"Huh..."

That sound like a pretty big deal. No one was sure what to say. Quite a reason to sympathize with a movie character...

Realizing she'd dragged the entire room down, she attempted to fix it.

"...Don't worry. She's a powerful mercenary. She's destroyed a few mobs in her time. I'm sure she's still alive."

"Y-yeah...you'll find her!" Lloyd exclaimed. "If there's any way I can help, just let me know!"

"...Master."

Phyllo and Lloyd were staring at each other tenderly.

Selen moved like lightning, forcing her way between them—like a professional basketball player moving too fast to be captured on-screen.

"And all the stonework in Rokujou is amazing!" she screamed. "I bet that movie really drives tourism!"

"It's a very different vibe from Azami. Going there would make you feel like an actor yourself!"

"I know! Eh-heh-heh. Sir Lloyd, we should go to Rokujou and re-enact scenes from the movie!"

Selen was just asking for a date, but Lloyd was oblivious to that sort of thing.

"I don't think I'm anywhere near as suave as that actor, though," he said.

"That's not true! You're just acting shy because everyone's watching." A generous interpretation.

Unaware of Selen's heavy breathing, Lloyd was talking about movies again. "Part of me really wants to be in a movie now!"

"I just care about the moola," Riho said. "How much do they pay actors?"

"……I could do an action scene."

"I know!" Allan agreed. "Mowing down enemies right and left, spouting a badass one-liner!"

"Even just being an extra would be fun. But I suppose they wouldn't want someone like me…," Lloyd said.

"If you were the hero and there was a love scene, I would do *anything* to wrest control of the lead actress role!" Selen exclaimed.

As they talked like any kids would, Colonel Choline—their teacher—came in.

"What, you're talking about movies?"

"You heard, Colonel Choline? Oh! I would love nothing better than to play Sir Lloyd's lover! Show everyone our love on screens around the world!"

"Good luck with that." Riho shrugged. "We're just cadets! Forget love scenes—no one would even want us in a movie at all."

But Choline's response caught them all off guard.

"But Rokujou's put out a casting call for extras from our military."
"""""What?!"""""

"Seems like they're using the production to advertise our alliance."
"""""What?!"""""

"Anyone interested, just sign this form! And since I'm from the Rokujou Sorcery Academy, I'm in charge of recommendations. I'll put in a good word for ya."
"""""What?!"""""

The shock of all this had clearly obliterated their vocabularies.

Choline made them all sit down, then explained the casting news from the top.

"So Rokujou and Azami are gonna make a movie together. I mean, script and schedule are all up to them, so we're just hopping on a movin' train."

This all sounded too good to be true.

"I get emphasizing our alliance as tensions rise with the Jiou Empire," Riho said. "But why do they want rank amateurs in a movie?"

"Well, it's an action movie," Choline explained. "And a pretty spectacular one. So they need good people on the stunts. That's why they're borrowing us, since we're used to getting banged up a bit."

This made sense to everyone. Their daily training was so rough-and-tumble, it would leave them ready not only for action movie stunt work, but possibly horror film territory, too.

They needed solid individuals and solid numbers. Volunteers, basically.

There was a strong undercurrent of disappointment: This meant the odds of them getting plucked out of the lineup and put in a lead role were extremely low. Allan looked especially crestfallen.

"Well, I figured as much," Riho declared, cleaning her ear. "Keeping labor costs down, huh?"

"Basically," Choline admitted. "They've already cast the main roles, but the supporting cast get their share of juicy moments, lines, or set pieces."

"…Oh?" Phyllo leaned forward. She wasn't about to deliver any dialogue, but action? She had that covered.

"And keep this on the down low, but that Amidine dude from *Rokujou Holiday*? He's the lead."

"He is?! The biggest star in all of Rokujou?! From *Rain Tomorrow* and *Heir to a Storm*?! *The* Amidine?"

Allan was getting a bit carried away. He knew all those titles off-hand? For all he pretended not to care, he sure was a bit of a fanboy… There's one of those in every crowd.

©Nao Watanuki

"My!" Selen gasped. "The suave lead in that wonderful film?"

The same lead you pasted Lloyd's face over, yes.

"Yup, so you may be extras this time, but you'll be working with Rokujou's biggest star, so who knows what doors that'll open?" Choline said.

The wheels in Riho's brain had started spinning.

"I could swipe his used dishes or trash... I bet that would fetch a pretty penny."

Riho was already in sketchy agency producer mode.

"It's free to join! You'll be in Rokujou for about two weeks total."

Choline handed out the stack of documents with all the details and then started the day's lecture.

But with the possibility of getting spotted by Amidine himself and making their debut on the silver screen, no one paid her any attention. All were lost in their fantasies, getting way ahead of themselves.

As for our hero, Lloyd Belladonna...

"An action movie?" He sighed, staring at the document.

Lloyd has enlisted in the army hoping to be a soldier like the hero of his favorite novel.

That soldier had been strong, but always helped those around him. Lloyd spent most of his time trying to live up to that ideal.

To be more manly.

To be cool.

Lloyd might look good in an apron behind the counter of the cafeteria, and students and teachers alike loved to crack jokes about what a great wife he'd be—and frankly, he'd got a lot of that back home in Kunlun.

But his inability to shake off the good wife vibe was starting to bother him.

In the Central District after school...Lloyd allowed himself to vent those feelings to Selen, Riho, Phyllo and Allan on his way home.

"I'm trying to be a cool soldier, but…it just feels like I'm getting nowhere."

"Don't be ridiculous! You're amazing, Lloyd! You've saved the country time and time again!"

Allan was specifically referring to the trouble with Jiou and the incident at the Reiyoukaku Hotel.

"Ah-ha-ha. Saved the country? Me? You're too funny."

Lloyd had, however, remained blissfully unaware of either. The idea that he was really weak was so permanently cemented in him that it was going to be hard to make him think otherwise.

When Allan proved unable to muster anything convincing, Selen took his place.

"Let me make this totally clear," she said. "Sir Lloyd—you're cool right now!"

That…was just another romantic confession, a calculated attempt to earn points with her crush by heaping praise upon him.

"Selen, Allan, you make a great comedy team."

It was dismissed as another joke. Selen's affections and aggressions both read as *girl who leads everyone on* in his mind.

"Team up with *him*…?" Selen hissed.

"Don't look so horrified!" Allan scowled back at her. "I ain't exactly thrilled to be lumped in with a crazy stalker."

"Heh-heh-heh. The best teams are built from like minds!" Riho cackled. "Anyway, Lloyd, don't worry about it."

She gave him a pat on the shoulder. Phyllo did the same.

"…Yes. It's the inside that counts."

This didn't seem to help much. "I'll try," he said. "Ah-ha-ha…I mean, 'inside,' I know I just have to keep working at it, but outside? I mean, I'm not getting any taller…"

"You're eating properly, right?" Riho asked. "The kids from my orphanage are all shooting up now that they've got proper food."

"Yes, I'm never picky. It just doesn't help. I even make sure to drink a bottle of milk after my bath every night and always do my calisthenics."

All the girls immediately pictured Lloyd in post-bath pajamas chugging milk and doing stretches…and every one of them thought, *Adorable!* None of them said this aloud, however. In his current frame of mind, that would only hurt his feelings.

"My fantasy repertoire has expanded!"

"…Just imagining it enriches the heart."

"Can't argue with that."

Allan immediately shattered the image.

"Lloyd, I do the bath, milk, calisthenics thing, too! We're the same!"

Now all the girls were picturing Lloyd in his pajamas *and* Allan with a towel around his waist (and not a full-size bath towel, just a tiny face cloth—the kind that gets a bit see-through when it's wet), doing stretches that displayed loads of butt crack.

"…" Riho unleashed a wordless dropkick.

"Gah! What was that for?!"

"Oh, please! Why would you tell us that now?! You're having us imagining all types of things!"

"Y-you mean you pictured me and Lloyd emerging from the bath togeth—"

CRACK.

Clean hit! A simple backhand slap from a mithril arm that made a very satisfying sound.

"'Ell, 'oyd, 'ere I 'o—"

"Allan, don't talk with your dislocated jaw."

"*Hngg*, gah!" Allan forced his jaw back in place, only shedding a few tears in the process. "Well, Lloyd, I'd better get going. If I'm gonna be in this movie, I figured I'd better stop by a bookstore and pick up a few books on acting!"

He then bowed way too low and was gone.

"He's *such* a fanboy," Riho grumbled.

"…You'd never know it looking at him."

"I bet in his mind, he's already a movie star with so many offers he doesn't know what to do. Someone tell him to stop counting chickens."

Coming from Selen—who spent most of her time imagining dates and marriage with Lloyd—this was rich. Riho and Phyllo glared at her.

They kept going up the gentle slope, soon reaching Marie's shop, where Lloyd lived.

"See you at school tomorrow!"

"Yeah. Don't worry too much, Lloyd."

"Thanks, Riho." He bowed and turned to enter the shop…

But no sooner had his fingers touched the knob than the door slammed open, and a pipsqueak of a grandma came barreling out, like a big dog that came racing toward the door before you could even say, "I'm home." That was Alka.

"You're back! Lloooooyd! It's been too long! How you've grown!"

They'd seen each other three days ago. Alka was always like this.

"Ah-ha-ha, you're here again, Chief?" Lloyd asked. "I haven't grown at all."

This last line sounded pretty gloomy. Alka had clearly touched a nerve.

Heedless of this—to be honest, the world's most tactless kid grandma had never heeded anything in her life—Alka started pulling clothes out of a sack.

"As much as I love how mismatched that military uniform looks on you, sometimes we gotta play to your strengths! Back to basics! Frilly aprons, shorts and suspenders, a cute little beret! I just couldn't wait to see that, so I brought them all here!"

Basics of what, exactly? Alka's eyes had turned to hearts, and she never saw the dubious looks the other girls were giving her.

"So once again…I'm just cute."

Lloyd would normally have laughed this off, but in his current mood, it was hitting him hard.

Figuring she should stop Alka obliviously breakdancing on a minefield, Selen whispered, "Chief Alka, now's not the time…"

"What, Selen?! You want to see it, too?! Lloyd covered in adorable frills!"

Alka wasn't listening.

"You, too, Selen? That's a low blow," Lloyd mumbled.

Framed for a crime she hadn't committed, Selen looked furious. She snapped instructions to her cursed belt. "Vritra, bind her!"

"As you wish!"

Vritra was the guardian beast of Kunlun, currently possessing Selen's belt. With a snap, the belt's length coiled around Alka.

"Wha— Hey! What's this for?" Alka struggled, but as she did, Marie appeared behind her.

"Master, no making scenes outside my shop! Oh, hello, everyone. Why is Lloyd so depressed? Was someone bullying him?"

"...Close enough," Phyllo whispered.

Forcing Lloyd to wear a frilly apron in his current mood was basically the same thing.

Marie had lived with Lloyd long enough to pick up on his mood instantly—a far cry from the village chief.

"Oh, Marie. We'll get you caught up on that front. Can we come in?"

"Uh, sure…"

"……And stay for dinner?"

Thus, the girls filled Marie in on current events while they ate.

The spread was magnificent. For a meal hastily thrown together for unexpected guests, the sheer variety on display definitely lived up to all those jokes back in Kunlun about what a great wife Lloyd would be… but better not bring that up *now*.

As they ate, the girls explained what had happened in class.

"We're all gonna be extras in a movie they're making in Rokujou," Selen clarified.

"Oh? That sounds amazing!" Alka cried. "I can't wait to see the costumes! Lloyd will totally be the sidekick, right? The world will know how adorable he is! Justice will be served! News will spread like wildfire— Mmph!"

As Alka jumped up and down, both feet on a land mine, the cursed belt tightened around her.

"Calm down, Master. So how does this connect to Lloyd's mood?"

"......Well," Phyllo said.

Please hold as they explain.

Meanwhile, Allan was at the bookstore.

"They *do* have books on acting! I'm basically a movie star already!"

You know how some people are satisfied just *buying* how-to books?

The explanation had concluded.

"Oh my goodness, I'm so sorry, Lloyd!"

A rare glimpse of the kid grandma prostrating herself. Marie's eyes were wide open, searing this image into her mind.

Alka was apologizing for her own stupidity so hard, she couldn't even get mad at Marie's.

"Oh, don't say that. You weren't trying to be mean."

Lloyd was in the kitchen, washing up...and wearing the frilly apron Alka had brought him. But...he wasn't turning around, so they couldn't see his face.

"Lloyd always looks you in your eyes when he speaks!" Riho cried, visibly worried. "If he's acting like this...it's not a good sign."

It was like having someone who normally fills their texts with emojis suddenly sending you a curt note in plain text. You were instantly like, "Oh, crap, what did I do wrong?"

"He's really in bad shape," Marie said, making sure Alka could hear her. "You can hear it in his voice."

Alka's apologies kicked up a notch, reaching the level of bowed prayer.

It wasn't clear if Lloyd registered any of this. For a long while, the only sound was the dishes clattering. Finally, he spoke again.

"After dinner, what was it? Shorts and suspenders? You want me to put those on, too?"

He sounded like he was just past caring.

A bead of sweat ran down Phyllo's cheek.

"……I've never seen him like this."

Lloyd made some tea, but the light in his eyes had gone out. He managed a listless smile.

"I know. Even as a movie extra, they'd never let me do any action. I'd just be part of a crowd, at best… Maybe forced into drag for a laugh."

"D-don't be silly!" Marie insisted. "The whole point of recruiting soldiers as extras is so you can do the action scenes! Stunts galore! So cheer up—Master, you say something."

Alka had quit genuflecting and had her arms folded, thinking hard.

"I've got it!" she cried. She flashed a sinister grin, then did her best to look dignified. "Lloyd, I owe you an apology. I've always doted on you like a grandson, and sometimes I forget you're no longer a cute little kid. Please forgive me."

"R-right…"

Forcing a grandson into a frilly apron against his will was definitely bordering on criminal levels of "doting," but putting that aside… Alka cleared her throat dramatically.

"However, an action movie? We have to admit that your height will place you at a disadvantage there. You may be an extra, but if you're significantly shorter than the lead actor, the audience will wonder why—it could be distracting."

"Master! Please, for once, take a hint! Ow!"

Alka's hand had lashed out and slapped Marie mid-reprimand.

"…Butt out. I have a plan," she hissed.

"This is something creepy again, isn't— *Hngg!*"

This time Alka grabbed her nose. Marie freed herself, but that nose was staying red for a bit.

Meanwhile, Alka's words had left Lloyd reeling in shock. He'd buried his face in his hands.

"I knew it…ugh…"

But Alka just kept piling on. "It's an unwritten law! To do action, you must be tall, nimble, and coquettish!"

That last word was generally just used for women and had nothing to do with action. She was talking shit again.

The girls all felt like she must be going somewhere with this and watched carefully.

Alka patted Lloyd's slumped shoulders with a very dubious grin.

"But, Lloyd," she said, "I knew this might happen. So I developed a very special rune just for you."

"Y-you knew this would happen?"

"That I did! So I invented the *grow-up* rune!"

Alka hit a dramatic pose so hard you could hear the Kabuki drummer hitting a beat. Everyone looked surprised.

"I don't blame you for reacting like that. But just you wait."

Alka dashed out the door and came back with a kitten. The mommy cat followed.

This kitten was maybe three months old and absolutely adorable... but Alka traced a rune on its side, charging it with magic.

"If I do this, even a tiny kitten will be... See for yourself."

There was a hiss, and smoke poured off that kitten...and then the cat was every bit as big as its mother. The mommy cat looked surprised and started yowling.

"...The mom is worried."

Alka dismissed Phyllo's concerns.

"Don't worry, it won't stay like this... Any second now..."

The kitten was dashing around the room, startled...but soon enough, smoke billowed out once more, and it was kitten-sized again. The mommy cat looked relieved. She picked her kitten up by the scruff of its neck and carried it back outside.

"With my current magic control in flux, I can only maintain the rune for three days max."

"R-runes can do *that*?" Lloyd seemed astonished.

Alka grinned like a con artist spotting an in. "Yes. I invented this just for you! And not because I wanted to dress up an adult version of Lloyd in a slick suit and make you pretend to work in a host club."

"That's definitely the reason."

"Absolutely."

"...Mm."

The back half was just a criminal confession.

She was *definitely* gonna play dress-up doll with an older Lloyd and get drunk off the sight of it.

Lloyd usually instinctively deflected this kind of nefarious scheme, but in his current condition? It was a snap decision, like seeing an infomercial just after your vacuum cleaner broke.

"Please! Use that rune on me! Make me into a real man!"

"Those are the words I wanted to hear! Straight to the bedroom—!"

Alka attempted to dive into Lloyd's chest like L—pin III, but Marie grabbed her collar. "Not what he meant!"

Lloyd blinked at them, baffled. "What other meaning is there?"

"It would take far too long to explain—I'll have to demonstrate!"

When the kid grandma kept her harassment going, Marie started getting genuinely angry.

"Not happening! Just use the dumb rune! Argh!"

"All right, all right, hold your horses. I'm working on it..."

Dangling by her collar, Alka turned toward Lloyd, using the same rune she'd used on the kitten.

Smoke started pouring out of him.

Alka held out her bag of costumes.

"Use the outfit in here!" she said. "Otherwise, your clothes will start ripping and tearing, which totally works for me—in fact, bring it on!"

"Not happening, Master! Lloyd! Back room! Quick!"

"R-right... Yikes, growing pains just hit my knees!"

Still smoking, Lloyd grabbed the outfit and scampered into the back room.

A silence settled over the shop. The only sound was someone gulping.

Finally, there was a creak as the door opened.

Footsteps came down the hall, and…

"Th-thanks for waiting… Are you sure I don't look weird?"

He was five feet, eleven inches. Around twenty years old.

Grown-up Lloyd Belladonna shifted uncomfortably in the clothing Alka had brought for him.

"Wow…"

"Wooow…"

"Woooooow!"

Marie, Selen, and Alka all applauded, cheering at the sight. He looked even better than they'd anticipated.

Riho's eyes had never opened wider. Her thoughts had short-circuited, and she was just soaking in the view.

Phyllo patted her on the shoulder. "……Mm."

She held out a hand for a shake.

Riho met her eyes, cheeks flushed, clearly overwhelmed. The two of them shook hands like businesspeople at the conclusion of a joint project, or two otaku realizing they have a *waifu* in common.

Cheers, applause, and handshakes… The vibe in Marie's shop was like a space program after a successful rocket launch.

Lloyd was just fidgeting uncomfortably, nonplussed by the whole thing. But this behavior in his new grown-up hot guy look was… appealingly unexpected.

"Master! I'm sorry! When you were ranting on about how a broken stereotype can instantly make someone more attractive, I thought you were being ridiculous, but this one really gets me right here!"

"Glad you're on board! Don't ever call me ridiculous! But just this once, I'll let you off the hook."

Alka and Marie threw their arms around each other.

©Nao Watanuki

"Er, huh? What's going on?" Lloyd said, sounding exactly like he always did.

This was so adorable that Selen was having trouble breathing. The noise from her throat was like the wind whistling through a crack in a window frame. Her expression was dangerously enraptured.

Even Alka, an experienced hunter of broken stereotypes, was struggling with the sight of a cool young guy acting like a flustered kid. Every fluid possible was pouring out of her face.

"Phoo…pho! Phoooooo! Pho!" she said in tones that would make even the most die-hard Vietnamese food fan cringe.

Lloyd took her hand.

"Um, Chief, thank you," he said. "If I'm this tall, I can definitely be in an action movie! As a cool extra!"

Handsome Lloyd's man-sized hands wrapped around Alka's little ones.

"Pho…"

She basically died of heart failure.

Her body hit the floor, looking like she'd accomplished all her goals in life. And she wasn't the first…

"Oh? Am I in heaven? What a lovely river!"

Selen was already dying nearby.

"You must not cross that river, Mistress!" Vritra cried.

Selen was thrashing like a fly just hit by bug spray (looking like she'd also accomplished all goals in life). Vritra was desperately calling her back from the shores of the river Styx.

Glancing at their corpses with a look that said, *What's got into them?* Lloyd stepped over to Phyllo.

"Ah-ha-ha, I'm actually taller than you now! That's new."

He looked down at her with a gentle smile, moving his hand from the top of her head to compare their heights.

"It's usually the other way around!"

Grown-up Lloyd's mouth was at the same height as Phyllo's.

Their breaths mixed together.

40

"Yes, usually-I'm-far-taller-so-anytime-I-fantasize-about-kissing-you-I-have-to-imagine-myself-bending-down-or-you-standing-on-your-tiptoes-struggling-to-keep-your-balance-but-this-is-something-that-had-never-once-occurred-to-me-ever-before-and-I-can't-bear-it—!"

Phyllo…broke character.

This was almost certainly a new record for longest line she'd ever uttered. And she'd blurted out some very revealing facts.

"Uh, Phyllo? Come back to us…"

Words came streaming out of her as if she were a broken-down robot. Riho grabbed Phyllo's shoulders and shook her.

"First the chief and Selen, now Phyllo? What's gotten into everyone? Is there something wrong with me?" Lloyd asked.

The natural womanizer had shot three of them down.

"Nope, nothing wrong! It's a huge success! Maybe too successful! What do we do, Marie? He's too different! We can't just claim he had a growth spurt!" Riho exclaimed.

Marie was clutching the last threads of her sanity, engaged in a desperate battle against Lloyd's hotness. Her knees clattered.

"It'll be fine, Riho! I have the authority to counterfeit any ID or paperwork we need!"

"Good job, Princess!" Riho shouted.

Lloyd was still blissfully unaware that Marie was the princess, so he just laughed.

"Good one, Riho! Marie's not a princess. She's the hero who saved the country from the shadows!"

He brushed his hair back as he spoke.

And when Marie saw that…

"Y-yeah…I'm free from all princess duties, free to be your princess alone…"

"Marie! You've gone off the deep end!"

Flames in her engine! A fourth plane down!

"Uh, Marie, what… Augh!"

Lloyd had taken a step closer, concerned, but his stride was longer than he anticipated, and he accidentally tripped over Selen's face.

"Huh?"

Lloyd had avoided falling by throwing his arms around Riho.

"Whoops! Sorry, Riho. Kinda hard to walk with these extra inches. Uh..."

"......Ahhh."

Yup, there goes the fifth.

Wrapped in his arms, a look of bliss on her face...Riho ascended into the column of light.

"Wh-what's wrong with everyone?"

The shop remained a mortuary for the better part of an hour.

"*Sigh...* Why do I gotta handle all the big jobs?" Choline muttered. It was early morning, but her eyes were already dead.

The sea breeze caressed her cheeks.

They were floating on the waters between Azami and Rokujou.

Early that morning, she had boarded a Rokujou-bound high-speed steamship on Azami's South Side, along with the soldiers and cadets who'd volunteered to be extras.

Everyone was on deck, chattering excitedly. Between their roles in the movie and the rare chance at a ride on a high-speed steamship, they were very excited. It was like this was a vacation. Choline herself had been excited until moments before—possibly more than anyone.

She hadn't worn herself out early. Every tour group has someone exhaust themselves, but this time, the cause lay elsewhere.

"I never thought Rokujou would be in such dire straits... I guess it makes sense to choose me, since I'm from there, but...I dunno if I'm cut out for it."

Back at the harbor, King Luke himself had briefed Choline on the true purpose of this excursion. The king of Rokujou, Sardin, had personally delivered a request for aid. His story read like the plot of a pulp novel. Choline had thought King Luke was joking and laughed in his face.

"I *wish* it wasn't true...but if they've booked a high-speed steamship, they mean business. Ugh, the pressure..."

She'd left the briefing still struggling to believe Rokujou was in *that* much trouble, but the choice of ship—she wasn't sure she'd even *seen* one of these before—had forced her to accept the gravity of the situation.

She let out another long sigh, staring at the waves below.

"And Chrome's on standby back home in case something goes wrong there... Rol's from Rokujou, too, but she's in exile... Mena's on vacation—I wish I was, too! I need time off, bad."

Griping at the horizon was just earning her sympathetic looks from the soldiers nearby, like she was a little kid who'd forgotten to pack any playing cards on a road trip and was struggling to get over it.

Riho and Selen came out on deck.

"All the rooms here are super nice! Yo, thanks for running the show here, Colonel Choline."

Riho waggled her fingers, then saw how distraught Choline was and moved closer.

"What's goin' on, Colonel? You drop your gummy bears overboard?"

"Don't be silly, Riho," Selen scolded. "She clearly forgot to pack a deck of cards."

"I've got those, Colonel Choline!" Allan offered. "We'll have to play Tycoon later."

None of these comments were helpful, so Choline just bared her teeth at them.

"It ain't that, ya clowns! Nah, fine, sure, sure, I dropped my gummy bears and cards in the ocean."

".........So clumsy."

"......I can't tell you the real reason, and, man, is *that* stressful."

Choline was under strict instructions to keep it to herself until she learned more about the request for aid. There were too many uncertainties right now, and they couldn't afford to make any careless moves—King Luke had said they should all act as if they really were just extras until the other side made contact.

Frustrated, Choline decided to ask Phyllo about Mena.

"Phyllo, why'd your sister have to take a long vacation *now*? Something come up?"

Phyllo cocked her head. "I dunno," she admitted. "…Even when we were mercenaries…she disappeared sometimes."

"Huh."

"…You don't need to worry about her, though. Why do you ask?"

"Oh, I just figured it would be a blast if she were along for the ride here! She's missing out! Such a shame!"

Choline was yelling at the water like the star of an inspirational drama.

"You sure brought a *lot* of extras," Riho observed, glancing around. "They're all volunteers, right? Bunch of fanboys."

"Riho," Selen said, "you're a bit of a fangirl yourself."

"Don't be silly! I've got my eye on other stuff. I'm gonna collect Amidine's used chopsticks or whatever and hawk that shit at massively inflated prices!"

"……That's worse," Phyllo said.

Riho ignored her. "Ha, scoff all you like! Oh, Micona and her crowd are here? Didn't think they were the type."

Her eyes had lit on a group of cadets whose armbands indicated they were upperclassmen. One of them was particularly dashing, a girl whose leadership qualities were every bit as impressive as her boobs. The head of the second-year students, Micona Zol.

When she saw Riho glancing her way, she advanced.

"Here she comes," Selen muttered. "Ready to challenge us to another competition, I bet. Clinging to outmoded ideas about seniority and the absurd belief that upperclassmen are always superior."

But Micona didn't seem to be in the mood. Her glare was more aggressive—downright angry.

"What's the meaning of *this*?" she snapped.

She was yelling already, but nobody knew why.

"Wanna explain yourself, lady?" Allan asked. "…Augh!"

Micona had kicked Allan in the shin as hard as she could. She was *really* mad.

Allan toppled over, and Micona breezed past him, glaring at the girls.

"Spill the beans! Secrets will do you no good!"

"Nobody has any clue what you're talking about."

Angrily barking questions and orders without subjects was just confusing everyone.

Micona suddenly collapsed in a flood of tears, as if they'd brought up a painful memory.

Once the initial deluge subsided, she managed to explain her anger, snot dangling from her nose.

"The other day, I was at Marie's shop! Hoping for a chance to peep in her bathroom win— *Ahem*! To catch her fresh out of the bath! I skipped all the way there!"

"The corrected version was almost as bad…"

This calls for an explanation. Micona Zol was not just another cadet; she was also madly in love with Marie. Her passion for Marie was the equal of Selen's for Lloyd—in superhero terms, Selen was the master of technique, while Micona was the master of raw power. One could call them the Double Stalkers. Oh, and the futuristic cyborg who fused technique and power? Alka.

"Just because you couldn't peep on Marie in the bath doesn't give you any right to take it out on us!" Selen declared. "Everyone knows most attempts at that end in failure! You must savor the lingering scents of a close call and consider yourself incredibly lucky if you catch a glimpse of Lloyd's flesh, or your mental sanity will never survive intact!"

"Your mind is long since gone."

Setting low-bar goals to attain a constant feeling of satisfaction was the key to any successful job performance. And, well, Selen's idea of a job was just *unusual*.

"That's helpful, Selen Hemein, but not the point! That's not my issue here!"

Selen's comment had been helpful? Oblivious to the concerned looks, Micona chewed on her thumbnail.

"Then what *is* your problem?"

"On that day, there was already no steam left in the bathroom. 'Damn, blew it again,' I thought and went around to the front window hoping to at least solace myself with a glimpse of Marie's smile."

"You do this, like, every day, then?" Riho asked.

"And…there was a strange man with Marie!"

"There was?"

"Yes! Early twenties, handsome, a gentle smile—chatting with her happily!"

At this point, the girls all figured out what had happened. Micona had clearly mistaken grown-up Lloyd for some sort of drop-in escort.

The girls all made faces, unable to just say, "That's Lloyd." No one wanted to explain.

Allan, however, had no clue what was going on. Rubbing his shin, he said, "Nice going, Marie."

Now Micona was kicking his other shin. Allan landed facedown on the deck.

"Don't say that! I thought Lloyd Belladonna was my only foe, but there was a dark horse candidate…and what they got up to…"

"……Details, please."

Phyllo's expression didn't waver, but there was a hint of anger in her voice.

"Marie—usually so refined! She said, 'At last, we're alone together!'" Micona explained. "She sat the man down, animal lust in her eyes… and began taking pictures! Clearly part of the visiting escort package!"

She'd likely been taking the headshots they needed for the forged documents. Everyone who knew better let this pass, but…

"She started normally, from the front, but then she stood next to him, taking shots of them together! Then she started making him pose!"

Marie had realized no one was watching and turned into a pinup photographer, taking things way too far.

"""""……Huh."""""

"And when she was done taking photos...then...then..." Micona wailed.

"Y-you can't stop there!" Riho yelled.

"I couldn't take it anymore and ran home sobbing! I didn't see the rest."

In actual fact, the photos had been more than enough for Marie, and she hadn't done anything else. She was fundamentally a wallflower.

But Micona's testimony cutting off at what seemed like a critical moment hit their fantasy-prone adolescent minds like a truck, and vivid images of what Marie might have done with grown-up Lloyd flooded every mind.

Just as the girls' faces reached maximum redness, Lloyd came back. He'd been staring at the ocean from the ship's prow.

"Boats are amazing! I mean, swimming would be way faster, but you can really enjoy the scenery on a leisurely trip like this. Uh, something wrong? Are you seasick?"

Nobody cared to say anything about Lloyd characterizing a high-speed ship as "leisurely." They all just looked grim.

"...Close enough, Sir Lloyd," Selen said.

"I feel pretty sick."

"......Mm."

The second she laid eyes on Lloyd, Micona advanced on him.

"Lloyd! Belladonna! What are you doing? Why aren't you watching over her?! It's your fault this home-visiting escort has his poisonous clutches in Marie!"

"Er? What are we talking about?" Lloyd said, looking lost.

"You fool! No, wait, Micona...stay positive. You can murder this escort in a back alley and then comfort a despondent Marie...heh-heh-heh. Turn this ship back to Azami!"

Little did Micona know the boy in front of her *was* this "escort"... and she would soon be face-to-face with him again.

Little did the girls know Marie was too much of a wallflower to have done any of the things they were imagining.

Speaking of which…

"Ah-ka-choo!"

"What is it this time, Marie? More dust? Or are you actually sick?"

"No, I think someone's just gossiping about me. I'm allergic to rumors."

"Well, good. Ready to head to Rokujou? A date with grown-up Lloyd abroad?!" Alka inexplicably held up a blindfold.

"I'm not supporting your date plans here, but…uh, Master? What's that for?"

"Well, we're gonna be flying there. And you're afraid of heights, so this'll help keep you from struggling. I'll gag and hogtie you later!"

"First I've heard of it! And I'm not afraid of heights! Anyone would be scared if you dragged them above cloud level! Mmph! Mmph!"

"Quit struggling! For safety concerns, I'm gonna fly real slow! It'll take all day!"

"Mm! Mmph! Mmaahh! If I'm that height for a full day, I'll literally die! Aaaaah!"

Thus, Marie's trip to Rokujou began with a screech of horror.

Little did she know an even more terrifying fate lay in store for her.

The ship made one stop at a port town on the border. It was just after noon on the second day…

"We're here, Lloyd! Long boat rides do take it out of you…"

Heedless of the concerns of those aboard, the high-speed steamship had arrived safely in Rokujou Kingdom.

"Wow! So this is Rokujou!"

The town spread out before Lloyd's eyes was made of stone—very different from Azami. It was the kind of city where any angle would make an amazing photograph. It had clearly captivated Lloyd's heart.

Meanwhile, a crowd had gathered, waiting for the cadets to disembark, all merchants hoping to peddle souvenirs or snacks.

"Yo, buddy, fancy some *manju?*"

"Get your Rokujou's famous sweet chestnuts here! They're roasted over Fire Magic!"

Choline pushed them all back like she was used to this.

"Okay, okay. Sorry, folks, we're here on business. Move along!"

Once sure no one was buying, they quickly vanished.

Allan stared after them, surprised by the aggressive sales. This didn't seem like that kind of town.

"It's like they got Azami's East Side and West Side mixed together," he commented.

"They do." Choline nodded. "You're on the money for once. Part of Rokujou's distinct flavor is how the genteel and the disreputable all are living right on top of each other. The upscale homes of the West Side and the slums of the East Side, all in the same place."

"Isn't that bad?" Selen asked.

"It was always the kind of place where financial interests and mercantile wheeler-dealers gathered. Once magic stones became big business, the government invested loads of money in magic research and turned themselves into the kingdom of magic. But at its roots, the whole country'll do anything for a quick buck. That's Rokujou! Let your guard down a second and some unscrupulous hawker will strip the hair off your butthole, Allan!"

"Colonel! I am not *that* hairy!"

Dropping more warnings, Choline led her students to their lodgings.

It was a large stone inn a short way down the coast with a view of the beach. It wasn't that far from town, but far enough the beach felt secluded. The cadets were very impressed.

"My, this isn't half-bad!" Selen noted.

"Yeah. I was expecting something even worse...," Allan agreed.

"Pfft, you nobles are such snobs," Riho scoffed. Selen and Allan were both from the families of local lords. "But why put a bunch of extras up somewhere nice?"

"Good question," Choline deadpanned. Fortunately, Riho was the only one looking this gift horse in the mouth. "Thank heavens everyone else is in vacation mode…"

If only she could be like them, blissfully ignorant. The colonel sighed for the umpteenth time that day.

"Colonel Choline, what should we do next? Stand by?" Lloyd asked earnestly.

Selen grabbed his hand, already carried away. "Obviously, this is free time! Come, Sir Lloyd! We must wander the winding streets of Rokujou, growing ever closer—!"

"You're getting a bit too free there, Selen. Do you want the cops here after you, too?"

"Yeah, you're representing the local lords and the Azami military! Restrain yourself for once!"

"…I'll show Master around. Don't worry. I know Rokujou."

Phyllo tried to pull Lloyd away, but Selen stopped her…by throwing her arms around him and rubbing her cheek on his.

"Selen! Phyllo! At least drop your things in your rooms first!"

As Choline yelled at them, a luxurious carriage pulled up in front of the inn.

The students turned to stare, and a man in a black suit stepped out, looking very dashing.

Well-groomed hair, gleaming with oils—oozing sex appeal. He walked like a hotshot businessman, the kind who sleeps with every female client or business partner.

"Pardon me, but would you be the guests from Azami Military Academy?"

"Yeah, we are but… Oh, y-you're…!"

Choline's voice went up a notch. Similar noises were spreading through the student body.

"Huh?"

"Oh!"

"That's…Amidine!"

"Wow! Amidine Oxo! Since his debut in *The Cotton Kerchief of Happiness*, he broke out big with *Rokujou Holiday*, but he's only thirty-five! What a star! Sir, can I have your autograph? Make it out to Allan."

One reaaaaally big fanboy here.

Amidine put a finger to his lips, silencing the crowd. He winked at everyone. How charming!

"Sorry, they're like this about everything," Choline said, remembering she was in charge. "But what brings a celebrity here?"

Amidine chuckled, scratching his neck. "You're in charge, then? I'm just running an errand at the whim of my director."

"The director?"

"Yeah, I've brought a message to all the extras from this film's director—Sardin Valyl-Tyrosine. He wants to start auditions, so he'd like you all to head to the location right away."

"A-auditions? Even though we're extras?"

"Well, more like a meet-and-greet. There's still a few named parts up for grabs, so some of you might end up filling those roles."

"W-wow," Choline squeaked out, surprised.

"Meet here in an hour," Amidine said, handing her a map. "Cadets and proper soldiers alike. Tell everyone!"

With that, he was gone.

"Auditions?" Choline muttered. "Wonder if this has anything to do with the request?"

"What request?" Selen asked.

"Oh, no, never mind that. All right! Stow your stuff, change out of uniform, and gather in the lobby! We got auditions to handle! Girls, make sure your makeup's on point! Guys, pluck them nose hairs!"

Meanwhile, Lloyd was giving himself a pep talk…

"It'll be okay… The audition's real sudden, but…I'll be nearly six feet tall!"

Anxiety and hope swirling inside, he got ready for the tryouts.

*   *   *

An hour later, they were outside an auditorium.

The audition hall was packed to the brim.

The building housed large meeting rooms and waiting rooms, which ordinarily hosted merchant conferences, lectures, and music lessons open to the public.

Now the place was swarming with soldiers from Azami. Even in street clothes, there were muscles bulging everywhere, and it was a pretty intimidating sight.

Allan was at the entrance, speaking confidently. He'd gone all the way, slicking his hair back with scented oils. If you lit a match, he would go up in flames.

"Right, Lloyd! Time for our first step toward silver-screen stardom!"

Allan brushed back his hair with an audible splat.

"R-right," Lloyd said nervously.

"Hmm, I see you're feeling the pressure. Never fear! I've got your back!" Allan thumped his chest, like just being there solved everything.

"Ah-ha-ha, I don't think you can watch each other's backs during auditions…"

"You've got his back?" Selen sneered. "More like you're holding him back! Sir Lloyd, we must show off our red-hot chemistry and get ourselves cast as a couple!"

She was just as bad.

Allan folded his arms, chuckling. "I've been studying up on acting the last few days! You sure you want to talk smack to a future movie star? I think you'd be better off getting my autograph now."

Riho immediately handed him a piece of paper. "Hey, future star! Sign this check! I've got, like, ten blank ones for you!"

"You're trying to screw over my future already?"

"………Mm," Phyllo agreed.

"Mm, nothing! Whatever. Good luck to you both!" Allan boomed. "I'm gonna go sign up and prepare myself in a waiting room! From this moment forth, we're enemies vying for the same roles! May the best man win!"

With a particularly overbearing grin, Allan sailed off inside.

"Lot of confidence for someone with his ugly mug," Riho said.

"......This is news how?"

"He always starts out pumped and loses his nerve the moment it gets real."

"......My point exactly."

They all knew Allan better than he knew himself.

Alka and Marie showed up soon after. Marie's blindfold was slipping off... Seemed like she'd got a panoramic view of the world above the clouds. She was almost as white.

"Nice crisp air up there! Oh, Marie, something ailing you?"

"...Master...you knocked the blindfold off deliberately..."

"Whaaat? I would neeeever."

This little grandma *definitely* had.

Lloyd saw them and waved. "Chief! Marie!"

"Oh, Lloyd! I heard you're auditioning. Here's your clothes for today!"

Alka gave him a linen bag. Swaying slightly, Marie handed him a card.

"Lloyd, here."

"This is... Oh, the fake ID! You took a new headshot for it so no one would guess I was using runes to look older!"

"Uh, yeah. Right."

Lloyd remained convinced everyone could use runes, and Marie had long since given up trying to explain. Gazing with wonder at his new ID, he realized something.

"Oh, there's no name on it."

Marie winced. "Yeah, well, you can't just use the same one, right? Lloyd, I figured you should pick it out yourself. Write whatever you like."

"Oh, really? Hmm..."

Lloyd folded his arms, not at all sure what to do. Some people spend over an hour thinking about this every time they start a video game, and Lloyd was probably one of these.

Selen leaned in with some advice. "If you need a fake name, put Hemein for the family name. A trial run for when you marry into my family…"

"You're such an idiot," Riho said.

Naturally, Selen had a lot of crap to back up her suggestion. "Come now, Riho. The best way to make a lie convincing is to mix in some truth! Anyone marrying into the family of a local lord will very likely be forced to take their name."

"The entire premise of this is wishful thinking…and we won't let it happen!"

Phyllo loomed over her. "…Then let's have him be my brother. We can be the three Quinone siblings."

"Forget the family name; we need a first name!"

Lloyd was caught at the center of a tug-of-war, but then Alka snatched the paperwork away.

"Hey, Master! There's only one of those! Don't doodle on it!"

"Fool, I'm not doodling! I'm cutting the argument short!"

Alka had written in a name.

Roy Akizuki.

Not a familiar sound at all.

"What? That's a weird name."

"Whatever, it's fine!"

"…Akizuki… An unusual combination of sounds. From the Domain?"

"Argh, time's a-wastin'! Let's do this!" Alka brushed off their questions, forcibly casting the rune on Lloyd.

Smoke started pouring off him.

"Wait, Chief! You can't just— Augh! Sorry, I'll go change in the bathroom!"

Lloyd rushed off—looking like a kid who had to pee.

A few minutes later, he came back a real man. Yeah, unfortunate phrasing. Let's just move past it, please.

"Thanks for waiting. Can you hold this for me?"

Hot Lloyd handed the bag of his old clothes to Marie.

"Gladly!" she exclaimed, still not used to him. She sounded like a female manager talking to the captain of the school baseball team.

"I've seen this sight already, but…" Riho trailed off.

"I can't get used to it," Selen said.

"……He's too hot."

Knowing the real Lloyd just made this grown-up version all the more appealing, and they were all weak at the knees.

"Mm! Lloyd, like we practiced, try speaking differently," Alka prompted.

"Right, to avoid anyone I know figuring it out, I need to sound cool, right?"

"Yeah, give the line I wrote you a try."

"Um… 'Don't worry. I'll never leave your side.'"

""""Gah!!"""""

"Er, is something wrong?"

Nothing. They'd just all had heart attacks.

"Hmm…well, best of luck…Roy."

"Thanks!"

The way Alka said "Roy" sure sounded like she was gazing at distant memories…

"Ugh, I hate feeling like this," Riho grumbled.

"This is how those middle-aged women who get addicted to host clubs feel!"

"…I feel like offering up tribute."

The other girls were too far gone to notice this change in Alka.

Marie smiled as Lloyd headed out.

"When he really is grown up, I can see him off like this every day… Huh?"

Phyllo had abruptly cut off Marie's vision with a blindfold…tying it very tight.

"……Mm."

"Phyllo? Why the blindfold—?"

Next, Selen's belt wrapped around the witch.

"Ha!"

"Wait, Selen?! Why are you tying me up?"

Then Riho growled low in Marie's ear. "Photos?"

"……How did you know?"

Marie's reaction gave the game away. No getting herself off the hook now.

"What photos?" Alka asked. It was not a word she could let go unnoticed. "Fill me in."

Selen told her everything…including a lot of completely spurious information provided by her imagination.

"I didn't do *that*!" Marie protested, but as she struggled, a photograph slipped out of her sleeve.

A picture of grown-up Lloyd and Marie together, their faces pressed together side by side, posed like a couple.

"You…dropped a photo there…"

"Crap! That one turned out *so well*, I decided it would cheer me up if I ever got depressed and have kept it with me ever since! Aughhh!"

The belt had gone a bit *too* tight.

"…She's guilty, Your Honor."

"Yep, guilty."

"Extremely guilty."

"Would you rather be dust or ash?"

Interrogating Marie made the girls late for the audition, but…they had only themselves to blame.

"Aughhhhhh! It was a moment of weakness!"

Same went for Marie.

Meanwhile, a wave of heat was radiating in a nearby waiting room.

It was like MMA fighters or professional wrestlers hyping themselves up for a match. You could almost see the flames.

Some were reading the audition script reception had provided; others were doing stretches—oh, someone's even doing vocal warm-ups.

"Aughhh! Let go! Get off me!"

"""Allan!"""

…Oh, it was just a bloodcurdling shriek.

Allan had entered the waiting room only to find a flock of drag queens—his ardent admirers—waiting in ambush. Most of the heat was radiating from them! It *did* seem rather fierce.

"It's been faaar too long, Allan! Are you here to be an extra?"

"Hey! Don't touch him there! And of course that's why he's here!"

"Why don't you join us, Allan? With those muscles, you'd be at the top in no time!"

"Seems unlikely! Thanks, but no thanks!"

Adult Lloyd stepped in, saw the commotion, and thought, *Man, Allan sure is popular!* Never change, kid. *Let me see. Anywhere still open? Oh, that corner's pretty empty.*

Lloyd found a corner left largely deserted—since no one wanted to push past the flock of Allan's fans.

Lloyd, however, slipped right on by.

"Mwa-ha!"

"Hey! Don't pinch me! No more pinching!" Allan roared.

The pincher took a step back…

"Oof! Sorry, honey…?"

…And he crashed right into Lloyd.

"Not a problem," Lloyd said, smiling. Then he turned to Allan. "Mind if I join you?"

He settled down on an empty seat.

There was a cryptic silence.

Lloyd started getting nervous. *Huh? Wh-what's wrong? Did I do something wrong? Did they recognize me?*

Lloyd thought his cover was about to be blown, but the admirers' concerns lay elsewhere.

He was hot. Very hot. And they'd all worked up a sweat fighting over Allan…

"Oh dear…"

"My, my…"

"I'd better go powder up!"

The entire pack raced off to the bathroom to fix their makeup. They would likely be gossiping about Lloyd in there, like the girls during a mid-mixer break.

With the drag division out of his hair, Allan turned to Lloyd.

"You there," he said.

"…Uh, yes?" Lloyd was trying to say as little as possible to avoid blowing his cover.

Allan slapped a hand on his shoulder, grinning from ear to ear.

"Thanks, dude! You deliberately jostled that shoulder to drive them off, right? You were a huge help!" Allan held out his hand.

Lloyd shook it, relieved his cover was intact.

"I'm Allan! Nice to meetcha."

"Roy…Akizuki."

"Roy, huh? You really saved my bacon there. They were getting all excited, pinching me in all the wrong places."

"…Sounds rough."

Lloyd wasn't talking much. Allan leaned in, peering at his face.

"Hmm? Say, are you…?"

"Urk!"

"Nervous? I know! It's a big audition! A huge movie!"

Lloyd's silence did read as stress. Allan folded his arms, nodding.

"Right, lemme see if I can pay you back! I'll tell you the acting fundamentals that'll help you nail any audition!"

Relieved his ruse was intact, Lloyd forgot himself, responding like he always did.

"Thanks a lot, Allan! That would be a big help!"

"Mm? You remind me of someone…"

"Erp… Well, never mind that."

"Yeah? Well, okay. Right, Roy, let me show you what I learned! Free of charge, least I can do! Teaching you will help me practice, too!"

Allan proceeded to give Lloyd a bunch of acting tips he'd read, like it was all from personal experience. Everyone knows the type: There's always someone at the office who's only been on the job a month but acts like a veteran the second a new hire shows up.

"First, even if you flub a line, don't stop to apologize. You only quit acting if the director yells 'cut'! It's vital to stay in character, keep the scene moving, and get through your lines."

"...Okay."

"Same with ad-libs, improvs, and études. The key there is to never say no to what your scene partner is doing. Going against the performance flow is just being selfish."

"Good to know."

Despite his enthusiastically pompous lecture...Allan had never actually acted.

Lloyd ate it up regardless.

Just as Allan ran out of tips, someone from the audition staff stepped in.

"Uh, if your number's in the thirties, please move to stand by in the hall. Remain absolutely silent so as not to disrupt the auditions in progress."

"Thirties? That's me. Roy?"

"Oh, me too."

"Nice! Let's get going. And remember, if you start freezing up, just imagine they're all potatoes."

Lloyd followed Allan out.

Whew, that was close. I wonder why everyone was so insistent that Allan couldn't know the truth? That's just making me extra nervous!

The reason was simple enough: Allan was a hopeless actor and would never be able to keep the secret.

But Lloyd was convinced Allan was a great performer, and nothing would ever dislodge this idea from his mind.

In the hall outside the audition room, applicants were seated in a row of chairs.

A group left the room, their auditions complete, and the next set of numbers was called. It seemed they were doing five at a time.

Hmm, no way to see what anyone else is doing... No, stay strong. I just have to act natural and do the best I can.

Lloyd relaxed a little, scanning his surroundings.

No one was doing vocal warm-ups out here. There were a few people gesticulating a bit, silently running through their lines.

And one person shaking like a leaf.

"I'll be fine... I'll be fine..."

That's right—Allan. As always, he was losing his mind right before his big moment.

"Er, are you okay?" asked Lloyd—Roy now.

"Y-yeah...this is...in excitement! Don't worry. They're all potatoes. Potatoes...and getting nervous here makes me worse than a potato... I'm sorry for everything..."

"You don't seem okay."

"Uh... No, sorry, don't worry about me. Man, this sure is different from pre-tournament nerves..."

"I'm scared, too," Lloyd admitted. "I've never done anything like this! Being jittery is normal. But you don't know what you can do until you try."

Allan blinked, looking up at him. "R-right... Good point, Roy. Heh. Man, you sound just like my master."

"Your master?"

"Yeah, his name's Lloyd. He's a little dude but really has it together. I'm proud to be his student."

At this point, the staff called out, "Next group, come on in."

Allan and Lloyd took a deep breath and went into the audition room together.

There was a long table at one end of the room with a panel of judges behind it, running pens across piles of paperwork. At the center of the table was a man with dark blond hair and an overbearing smile. He waved the applicants toward a set of chairs.

"'Sup, everyone, the name's Sardin. Loosen up! Don't go stressing it just because I'm the king. Make yourselves at home."

He winked hard enough it made a *ding*, confusing everyone. What? This was the king of Rokujou? Make themselves at home? He was really gonna set the tone like this?

Next to Sardin was an extremely calm man with black hair—Amidine. He wore a top-class suit, rifling through documents like a veteran military strategist preparing for war.

When he saw everyone looking confused, he turned to Sardin.

"Your Majesty, you're out in public. Introduce yourself properly."

"Sorry, I've had to do this for every group! Guess I cut it a bit too short! Not like I'm lacking in ways to introduce myself or anything—I've got an endless supply!"

"No matter how many times you've done it, this is their first time meeting you. You have a royal responsibility to do it right."

"Fair enough. My name is Sardin Valyl-Tyrosine. I'm the king of Rokujou and the director of this motion picture. Better?"

"Don't ask me...," Amidine grumbled. He finished going over the documents and looked up at the applicants.

"My name is Amidine Oxo," he said, flashing a dazzling smile. "I'll be playing the lead role in this film."

"The real Amidine is something else! Just sitting in a chair, and you can tell he's a star!"

Sitting or standing didn't make much difference, really, but it didn't take much to impress a fanboy.

Sardin shot Allan a slight frown.

"You seem more impressed with *him*! That's enough to make a man royally jealous! As a king should be."

"I *am* an actor," Amidine said. "If you turn this movie into a hit, you might find yourself equally famous."

"Good point, Amidine! That's why I want to make this movie work.

With your help!" Sardin beamed at the applicants. Then he got down to business. "You on the left, step forward."

The soldier in front of Allan stepped forward nervously, bowed, and began reading the script.

Sardin grinned the whole time. Amidine didn't bat an eye, but his pen ran across the page, clearly checking things off. This rattled the soldier... It was hard to keep acting when no one responded at all.

At last, he reached the end of the script, and Sardin asked a few questions. Some small talk ensued, followed by a few things about his postings in the army, etc.

"Hmm, thanks. Take a seat."

The soldier let out of a sigh of relief and sat down.

"Your Majesty, keep the small talk to a minimum," Amidine suggested.

"You've got to get to know them, Amidine!" Sardin protested, beaming. "Especially with amateurs—they'll be at their best playing themselves."

"The whole point of acting is to be convincing in any situation...but you have a point."

"I know! Next!"

Allan leaped to his feet. "Yesh!"

Amidine flinched like someone had dropped an ice cube down the back of his shirt.

Sardin glanced at the documents, enthusiastically reading them aloud. "Hmm, Allan Toin Lidocaine! So you're the famous dragon slayer who can summon legendary heroes!"

"Yesh!"

"......Uh, hmm. Well, best of luck!" Sardin was starting to look worried. He pointed at the script in Allan's hands.

"Yesh!" Allan said, several times, like a broken record. Then he finally started reading.

A few minutes later...

"I'm a failure... A hopeless shell of a man..."

Allan collapsed in his chair, hanging his head, white as a sheet. A burned-out, hollow husk, he looked like he'd blown his life savings at the racetrack or had his marriage proposal brutally shot down.

Amidine scratched his head with his pen. "Never seen anyone apologize for every blown line…"

And Allan had blown his apologies and apologized for that, stressing his lines so hard his intonation was all over the map. The script was supposed to be a routine conversation, but Allan read it like an elementary school student reading their essay aloud. In other words, it was a disaster.

It was the inevitable fate of anyone who thinks they can act just because they read a book about it.

"Oh no…if a man like Allan goes down in flames… Professional auditions are serious business!"

Allan's brutal death had definitely scared Lloyd.

"That was rough, Your Majesty."

"Well, he can probably handle the action, maybe? Next!"

"That's me… P-present!" Lloyd redirected his energy and shot up from his seat, bowing to Sardin and Amidine.

"Well, you've got good manners…"

But something was off. Sardin looked down at Lloyd's paperwork and froze.

"Um?" Lloyd said, looking up from his script.

Amidine looked equally puzzled. "Something wrong, Your Majesty?"

"…Uh, no, nothing! Er, Roy, was it? Mind if I start with some questions?"

"Uh, sure."

"If someone from another country was in trouble, what would you—as a soldier of Azami—do about it?"

This sure came out of nowhere. Lloyd blinked at him.

"King Sardin, what kind of question is that?"

"Never mind, I'm just curious."

"Well," Lloyd said. "It doesn't matter if they're a citizen of Azami or not. I'd do what I could to help. I became a soldier to help people, after all."

"Oh? That's good to hear." Sardin sounded impressed.

Completely lost, Amidine waved a hand. "Your Majesty, this is an audition, not a job interview."

"Fair enough! Go on and read your lines— Mm?"

There was a commotion from the hall.

"What the— Huh?!"

Even as Amidine spoke, the door slammed open, and a woman burst in.

"Hahhhhh…hahhh…there you are!"

It was Micona. Selen, Riho, and Phyllo were all right on her heels, trying to stop her.

"Micona, stop! What are you doing?!"

But Micona shook off Selen's belt, her breath so ragged she sounded like a monster. She advanced on grown-up Lloyd, snarling.

"Isn't it obvious?! Your fate is sealed, home-service escort! I never thought you'd be a soldier, and auditioning here!"

Micona thought grown-up Lloyd had seduced Marie and had been unable to stop herself from kicking the door in. She was clearly in no mind to listen to any explanations.

"What a mess," Riho whimpered. "Restrain her before she makes this worse! I don't care if you have to skin her alive!"

"…It's all Marie's fault," Phyllo grumbled, punching Micona.

There was a sharp snap as her fist sliced the air.

Weeping bitter tears, Micona had managed to dodge it.

"Don't stop me! I'm gonna kill him and snare Marie on the rebound!"

"What a terrifying face and suggestion!" Selen wailed. "I can't believe you're even human!"

Riho scoffed. "Like you're any better."

Phyllo was still swinging, driving Micona back—toward the table where Sardin and Amidine sat.

"You soldiers sure are spirited… Oh?"

"Don't stand there looking impressed, Your Majesty! Augh!"

Phyllo's dropkick had snapped the table in two.

"……She dodged me."

Paperwork filled the air like confetti. Grinning, Sardin said, "What's your name?"

"……Phyllo."

"Your last name?"

"…Quinone. Phyllo Quinone."

"Hmm…well, I love your energy!" He grinned, suddenly *very* happy.

"Why are you hitting on her, Your Majesty?!" Amidine wailed. "Stop them!"

"Ha-ha-ha, I'm not hitting on her, Amidine! Oof!"

Phyllo had just used Sardin's face as a stepping-stone to take a flying leap at Micona.

"Don't get in my way, Phyllo Quinone!" she barked.

"……You stand before the king. Rudeness must be stopped with force."

"You were *way* ruder!" Riho shrieked. "You stepped on him!"

Sardin's face was certainly quite red, but his grin never wavered.

"Ha-ha-ha! So much energy! I love it!"

"Seriously? You're way too generous…"

Selen managed to get her belt around Micona at last, restraining her, but the auditions were canceled, and the soldiers were sent home.

"…You couldn't have done that *before* my audition?" Allan muttered.

That evening, as the sun set over the Rokujou shopping district… Lloyd, still grown up, was walking through the streets, mingling with the post-work crowds.

Obviously, he was not here to take advantage of his adult body to get involved in all manner of previously unexplored R-rated pleasures.

"Hmm…the auditions ended early. The chief and Marie aren't here yet…"

Thanks to Micona's disruption, Lloyd had been left with some unexpected free time and found himself wandering around aimlessly.

Marie was holding his usual clothing. If he went back to the inn looking like this, everyone except the girls would be surprised, and Micona might fly off the handle again…

Heedless to the calls of the nightclub doormen, Lloyd wondered how to fill the time.

Then a man came sidling up to him. He was dressed like a craftsman's apprentice, but something about him seemed…not like the others.

This guy was clearly up to no good.

When he approached Lloyd…he tried to slip a piece of paper into Lloyd's pocket with professional ease.

In a crowd this size, no one would notice. Normally.

But Lloyd was anything but normal and grabbed the man's wrist just in time.

"Huh? What's up?"

"How?!" The man glanced at his wrist in shock but quickly recovered. "So he was right about you… Didn't think you'd clock me before I slipped you the letter."

"Clock? Letter?"

"Sorry—this letter's from *him*. It's about the job, Roy Akizuki."

"Him? Job?"

The man tried to lead Lloyd away. Lloyd forgot who he was supposed to be.

"Uh, sorry, I'm confused. And I'm not supposed to go anywhere with strangers… I could get in trouble."

This was a line that would be totally natural coming from Lloyd in his normal state—but not from a man in his early twenties. It sounded like something a kid would say, so the man laughed out loud.

"Heh-heh, you're acting pretty funny, there… Er, pardon me."

Acting? The wheels in Lloyd's brain started turning.

The way this man had slipped him the letter was like something in a movie. So was the line about a mysterious "him" and "the job." And if this guy knew him as Roy Akizuki…

Is this an ad-lib? Improv? He's an actor!

Not at all.

But Lloyd's boundless capacity for positive thinking was carrying him further from the truth.

I see! The audition isn't over yet! They just made it seem like it was canceled, but that was a trick! They wanted to see how adaptable we are! I thought they gave up weirdly fast!

This was totally wrong, but Lloyd was now convinced this was the *real* audition.

The grin on his face was taken as acceptance.

"I'm glad we have come to an understanding. He's waiting for you… This way."

Lloyd remembered Allan's advice.

"The key to improv is to never say no to what your scene partner is doing. Going against the performance flow is just being selfish."

I have to follow along! I'd better go where he tells me.

"Sure," Lloyd said, lowering his voice theatrically.

Following Allan's advice…he trailed behind the man.

Lloyd soon found himself in a narrow back alley, far from the main drag. He was taken into a bar that just screamed *secret lair*.

The bartender and customers were all sizing him up…which made Lloyd nervous.

He looked around the room. It was really dark and ominous—not much like any bar he'd seen.

The wall was decorated with swords, shields, and muskets, and there was a map of Rokujou spread out on a table. This looked like a military briefing room, which surprised Lloyd.

Weapons? Why?

Everyone here had clearly survived far more battles than your average barfly. And from the looks they gave him, they obviously weren't stopping by for a pint after work.

Uh…what's going on? He braced himself.

"Surprised?"

This voice came over the back of a chair behind the table. There was a man sitting in it, and he swung around to face Lloyd.

"Y-you're…!"

It was King Sardin Valyl-Tyrosine, from the audition hall.

There was no trace of his former goofiness—now he radiated solemn dignity.

"Yes, I am Sardin. Thank you for coming, Roy. Have a seat."

Lloyd did as he was told, quietly seating himself. But inside…

See? I knew this was all part of the audition! An improv! King Sardin's acting totally different, and there's guns and props on the walls!

…Like always, Lloyd was entirely misreading the situation.

"This may be a bar, but I'm afraid what we have to discuss is too grim to offer you a drink. My apologies."

"Don't worry, I can't drink anyway."

He might look grown up, but he was just a kid. Lloyd would never drink alcohol.

"Hmm," Sardin said, muttering under his breath. "I suppose in your line of work, you can't risk drinking anything you don't bring yourself."

His eyes bored into Lloyd.

"The king of Azami really stepped up—not just sending the elite cadets, but a professional like yourself."

"The king? Professional who?"

Sardin took the blank look on Lloyd's face as playing dumb.

"Ha-ha-ha, no need for the act." He chuckled. "I know the king sent you here personally."

Sardin produced the fake ID Lloyd had brought with him—the one Marie made.

"Look closely. It's well-crafted, but the ID number is a dead give-away; you aren't that young! Yet this seal is real. In other words, this is a fake ID, but one made under direct royal supervision. A hidden message only another king would understand."

Wow, he's even using props to make his performance seem real! And he told that whopper about royal supervision so easily!

That was because he was totally right about the origins of the document in question...but to explain that to Lloyd, they would first have to prove Marie was the princess.

Sardin tossed the ID over to Lloyd, who was once again impressed with the king's talent for ad-libbing.

Mindful of Allan's advice—never say no—Lloyd did his best to play along.

"Well done, Your Majesty... So, assuming I am sent by Azami...why have you called me here?"

His voice quiet and grim, Sardin began to explain. "Rokujou is in serious trouble."

"Hardly seems like it," Lloyd observed, struggling a bit with the register of his voice. "Seems like these movies are really keeping business booming."

"Perhaps that's what it looks like from the outside, Roy." Sardin shook his head. "But that money isn't going anywhere legitimate."

"Oh?"

"Everyone's got their hand in the pot. Skimming off the top, calling it fees to use for their technology or materials...or just blatantly going right into the pockets of the middlemen. Safe to assume all that money is actually headed straight to Jiou."

"So Jiou...is siphoning your profits?"

"Yeah. A certain organization at the heart of Rokujou Kingdom is controlling everything and funding the Jiou Empire. It's got to the point where Rokujou exists in name alone." Sardin suddenly looked very tired. "They've got all reaches of the government under their thumb...and I'm afraid they've even figured out my weakness."

"What organization is this? And what have they got on you?"

"A crime syndicate known as the Rising Blue Dragon. All our government policies are designed to enhance their profits. Weapon manufacturing and smuggling...arming and supplying extremist groups...even using necromancy to loot and pillage. We're turning a blind eye to it all."

"Necromancy?"

"Yeah, if you don't fork over the protection money, they'll make spirits possess family members, causing them to kill one another. And turn the dead into zombies, which attack...and that's not something we can let slide!" Sardin clenched his fists in fury.

But the situation he'd described was so grim that Lloyd thought...

Wow, he has to be acting. There's no way this is true.

The more Sardin talked, the more convinced Lloyd was.

Sardin took a deep breath, calming himself...and gestured to the crowd around him.

"I trust every man here. The Rising Blue Dragon have taken everything from them. Family, jobs... We're the resistance. The idea of a king leading the resistance sounds like a bad joke, right?"

When he heard the word *resistance*, Lloyd glanced at the swords and muskets, thinking, *Oh, so that explains these props.* They're all real, though...

Then he saw a familiar figure leaning against the wall. Amidine.

"Him, too?" Lloyd asked.

Amidine nodded. "Most of the film staff are Anti-Rising Blue Dragon members. We're using the movie as cover to gather weapons—passing them off as props. And our location scouts are actually monitoring their activities, locating their hideouts."

It must be hard to dream up this stuff on the spot—but I guess you can't be a movie star without learning to improvise!

"And the movie was the perfect cover to bring in reinforcements from Azami." Sardin grinned. "Your king is a wise man—from a few short lines, he knew exactly what we needed. We called it an audition, but elite forces like Allan Toin Lidocaine and Micona Zol? That's the kind of backup we need."

"We'll be filming for two weeks," Amidine added. "We're hoping that's enough time for you to wipe the Rising Blue Dragon out. Can you do it, Mr. Akizuki?"

By way of response, Lloyd stole a line from his favorite novel.

"If I didn't have confidence, I wouldn't be in this line of work."

"Well put... Looking forward to working with you."

"Any specific instructions? I'm sure you aren't just leaving it all to me... Are you?"

Sardin handed Lloyd a photograph.

A blond woman was glaring at the camera.

"Who is she?" Lloyd asked, glancing it over.

"Her name's Ubi. She should prove essential to discovering their hideout. Start by securing her. She's...my wife."

"No need to tell him *that*," Amidine snapped, annoyed.

"It's best to be up-front about these things, Amidine," Sardin said bitterly. "That's what brought us to this. My failure to tell the world about her is the direct cause of our current predicament."

"Argh." Amidine shook his head. "Mr. Akizuki, not a word of this to anyone until the matter is resolved." He placed a finger to his lips with a wink.

So cool, Lloyd thought. Realizing he was slipping out of character, he clutched at straws, trying to keep the improv going.

"Uh, right...of course." Lloyd glanced down at the photo in his hand. "If you want her secured, does that mean she's imprisoned somewhere?"

Sardin nodded gravely, then clarified. "Not imprisoned...but an artifact has robbed her of her freedom. We've approached several times, but she always flees. She often appears in this vicinity in the dead of night... Here, take this. You'll need it to secure her personage."

Sardin took an old pendant out of his pocket and handed it to Lloyd.

"You found it, Your Majesty?" Amidine asked, his eyes going wide.

Sardin grinned. "Sorry for the late warning, Amidine. It was discovered in the things we bought from that merchant. I had a hunch…and that is the Saint's Pendant. Since ancient times, it is said to have the power to banish evil spirits… It can counter the Jewel of Legions."

"We're supposed to be sharing information, Your Majesty."

But there was a grin on Amidine's lips.

"Ha-ha-ha, hadn't you heard? Kings are notoriously bad at that."

"News to me."

Watching these veteran "actors" go at it, Lloyd carefully placed the photo and pendant in his pocket.

"Well, Mr. Akizuki," Amidine said, turning back to him. "Your mission is to free her, take her to safety, and locate their lair—and with the backing of the Azami forces, wipe them out for good. Can you do it?"

"Of course. How does this pendant work?"

He held it up in front of him. A simple pendant, but in the lantern light, it took on a sinister glow.

"Well…it's a pendant. I suspect you need to place it around her neck. The merchant said something about swinging it around, but…that makes no sense. Why make it a pendant, then?"

"Yeah, nobody would swing a pendant around."

A very reasonable set of arguments. After all, nobody normal would ever think to do that. The only problem was…the person who made this wasn't normal.

"First, find Ubi and use that pendant to lift the curse. Please, Roy."

"Very well," Lloyd said theatrically.

Amidine glanced up at the clock on the wall. "Your Majesty, it's time."

"Already? I'd better get back to the castle before anyone gets suspicious. Gotta act the fool again!"

"Act? That's at least half-real! Nobody can act that dumb without a core of true stupidity."

"Says the movie star."

These two bickered like old friends. *Like something out of a real movie*, Lloyd thought. *Even in an improv, they can trade cool one-liners!*

"Roy."

"…Uh, yes? I mean, what is it?"

Sardin rose to his feet and bowed low. "I must be going. I'm glad this discussion was so productive."

Lloyd took this to mean the improv was over and snapped back to his usual self.

"Oh, okay! Good work, everyone! Thanks so much!"

"Er…uh, sure?"

Lloyd was suddenly acting like a totally different person, and both Sardin and Amidine looked surprised. Lloyd had already moved over to the wall, however, poking the swords and guns with great interest—inspecting the props.

"Heh…these are really well-made!"

"Uh…Roy?"

"Oh, yes! Well, I'll see you tomorrow, Director!"

Seeing this transformation, Sardin said only one thing. "You're such a professional! I expect great things."

"Huh?" Lloyd looked confused, never connecting this to all that acting they'd just done.

Amidine patted him on the shoulder. "Mr. Akizuki, I'll walk you to the main road. All these winding alleys must be a maze to someone new to the city."

"Oh, thanks, that would be really helpful!"

"You really turn on a dime, huh? You could be a great actor."

"Oh, really? Thanks!"

Amidine led Lloyd out the lair of the Anti-Rising Blue Dragon.

A short walk away, Amidine pulled out a match and lit a cigarette.

It was very dark here. The streetlamps didn't reach this corner. The only light on their faces came from the tiny flame.

The scent of the match and the ensuing cigarette smoke tickled Lloyd's nose.

He coughed lightly. He was a kid inside. No one around him smoked.

"Oh, sorry, mister. Should have waited till we were in the open."

"Oh, it's fine," Lloyd said.

But Amidine looked genuinely regretful. "I just gotta have a smoke before I work."

"Oh? You still have work? Wow."

Lloyd was just worried about late hours, but Amidine winced.

"Yeah, well... Sometimes I wish I didn't have to be Amidine Oxo all the time. If I could be someone else, go far away... That might be a weird thing for an actor to say."

He took a drag on his cigarette, then scratched his head sheepishly.

"Mind if I take a look at that pendant? I'm worried someone foisted a fake off on him. Oh, and can I see the photograph, too?"

Lloyd happily handed over the photo and pendant.

In the dark alley, Amidine used the light of his cigarette to inspect the pendant.

Like a detective poring over evidence. Totally nailing the hard-boiled cop vibe.

"Damn...it is real."

"Is that bad?"

"Mm? Oh, never mind, mister."

They walked on. They saw lights ahead.

Lloyd wondered if they had reached the main road, but instead...he found himself in a harbor filled with freight ships. Waves lapping, the sea breeze brushing past them.

"Huh?" Lloyd said out loud, looking at Amidine. "Does this lead back to the main street?"

As he turned, something struck him in the chest.

The smell of smoke, not from the cigarette.

Lloyd looked down and found a small hole in his chest. He looked up at Amidine and saw a pistol in his hand.

He'd been shot.

Confused, Lloyd stared at Amidine, his expression asking, *Why?*

"You look like you have questions, mister."

"Y-yeah."

"But the answers are simple. This is my job. As the boss of the Rising Blue Dragon."

"Y-you mean…?"

"The resistance Sardin's leading? The whole thing only exists to keep tabs on him. Poor fool's dancing on the palm of my hand. But I'm impressed he managed to make a deal with Azami at the Reiyoukaku without us noticing. He's craftier than he looks."

Amidine pointed his gun at Lloyd again.

"This is good-bye. See you in hell when it's my time."

A ship whistle rang out.

And so did his pistol.

The bullet went through Lloyd's chest—and he fell backward into the ocean.

Amidine crouched down on the wharf, taking a drag on his cigarette as he watched the water where Lloyd had fallen.

"Unpleasant work," he grumbled. "Two to the heart… You gotta be a monster to survive that."

He held up the pendant he'd stolen, inspecting it in the moonlight.

"Can't believe he really found it. The Saint's Pendant… Well done, Your Majesty."

Then he looked at the photo.

"All for the love of a woman, huh? That's all it takes to drive a man."

Some time passed.

"No signs of the body surfacing… Must have been caught by an undercurrent."

Amidine put the pendant in his pocket, certain Lloyd was dead. Then he flicked his spent cigarette into the water.

A figure emerged from the shadows, like he had always been there—like he was part of the scenery.

"Hi there!"

He had the pleasant breeziness of a captain on shore leave or a warehouse janitor.

"You're—," Amidine began.

A cheery young man with a black backpack and a deep tan stepped out from behind the older gentleman.

"'Sup, movie star! How's it going?"

"Fine," Amidine grumbled, looking tired already. "Shouma, Sou... how long have you been here?"

The older man—Sou—smiled faintly. "Mere moments," he admitted.

Shouma started firing questions at Amidine like a tabloid reporter.

"Just wanted a progress report! I mean, you taking photos of the king's directing work? We're sponsoring this deal! We wanna know it all!"

"I said it's going fine. Between the acting and the crime boss, I've got this country wrapped around my finger outside and in."

"Splendid," Sou said.

Amidine looked displeased. "Why are we working so hard to popularize movies? If you just want to line Jiou's pockets, there's way more efficient ways to make money."

This was a reasonable question. But the response?

"Isn't it obvious?! We wanna see Lloyd in action! Have the whole world watch, and the whole world know he's here to save them!"

"Film is unshakable evidence. We are the root of all evil, and Lloyd will stand against the threat we pose the world. In a movie. That will finally free me from the yoke called hero."

"Which is why we gotta release all the demon lords, right, Sou?"

"Release them, and have Jiou conquer the world... We've had our setbacks, but all manageable."

"...Right," Amidine replied. He didn't know who Lloyd was or what that "yoke" crap meant, so their explanation was clear as mud.

It was like being pitched a plot filled with jargon and made-up terms. Amidine nodded like a student pretending to follow along in class. These two *were* his sponsors, after all.

The two of them jabbered on about how great Lloyd was and what

©Nao Watanuki

future developments lay in store. When they were satisfied, they turned to Amidine.

"Anyway, we're gonna go eat some offal stew."

"Looking forward to the movie!"

And with that, they vanished into the darkness.

Having to deal with their inane chatter right after the unpleasantness of murder left Amidine with a towering rage and nowhere to unleash it.

"Was this ever what I wanted to do? Damn it all."

Amidine swore, but the boat whistle drowned it out, and no one heard him.

…And yes, shortly after Amidine left, Lloyd popped out of the water like nothing had happened.

"Amidine! Huh? He's gone!"

Lloyd clambered onto the wharf, wrung out his clothes, and looked around.

The harbor was deserted.

"Oh dear…I had no idea the improv was still going! But I guess it was."

He scratched absently at the bullets embedded in his chest, looking remorseful.

"That gun prop is amazing! It doesn't hurt at all, but this blood looks so real!"

Because it was real? Like it's a real gun?

Lloyd sighed. "Amidine was waiting for me to surface. He must have thought I was an idiot for staying down there and got tired of waiting to see what I'd do next. Maybe I was supposed to go on the offensive?"

Amidine did not think Lloyd was an idiot, on the grounds that nobody can actually hold their breath that long.

"No point in fretting over it now! I just have to be a better extra tomorrow! Oh! It's so late! The chief and Marie will be waiting for me!"

Lloyd shook himself like a dog, and his clothes were instantly dry. No normal human would ever be able to dry their clothes like that, but at Lloyd's level, you're as good as the spin cycle on your average washing machine. Little-known fact!

He trotted off toward the main road, where Alka and Marie were getting sick of waiting for him.

Meanwhile, in the shopping district of Rokujou...stallkeepers were barking in the rapid-fire local accent, selling all kinds of food—rice, noodles, foreign delicacies, you name it. These shops didn't care if you didn't normally top *manju* with custard, deep-fry 'em, or serve 'em with donuts; if it sold more, they'd do it, no questions asked.

Alka and Marie were at a noodle shop, slurping offal stew. Soy sauce–based soup, gooey offal, crisp veggies, and burdock. It was great.

"We need him to eat this so he can make it for us later," Alka said, grinning ear to ear.

"It's good, but...my mouth is still stinging..."

Marie had bandages plastered all around her face and was scowling at her food.

"Just punishment for pushing your luck! Be glad you got off so light. Taking photos like you're a couple..."

"I have no excuse."

"I've moved on...but this is an odd kingdom. They'll take in anything popular and make it their own. I guess you can call them open-minded."

Alka glanced around at the people and buildings.

"Probably why Eug targeted them."

A shadow passed over her face.

"You mean the movies?" Marie asked, swallowing her offal.

"Yeah. By all rights, motion pictures won't become a thing until civilization is a lot further ahead."

"Even still photos are really expensive."

"And even those are ahead of their time... Same with telephones.

Eug's twisted ambitions are showing up all over. And Sou and Shouma are mixed up in it."

Marie took a sip of tea, remembering what Eug had said.

"I'll force this world to develop itself...and the demon lords are just one means to that end."

The demon lords provided the threat. When humans found themselves in trouble, they'd accept the anachronistic weapons Eug offered.

"She's laying the groundwork, making people more willing to accept advanced technology."

"But, Master, the world progressing isn't inherently bad. War with the demon lords is, of course, but..."

But making people's lives better was a good thing.

"No, Marie," Alka argued. "The problem is what lies beyond that—with Eug's real goal."

"Her goal?"

"Yeah. Inside the Last Dungeon..."

But before Alka could reveal the truth...

"Wow, these stalls are so international! That's what I call passion!"

"Then maybe we should eat something entirely new. This offal stew, perhaps?"

Talk about a coincidence! Shouma and Sou were sitting at the next table.

"Ah!"

"Ah!"

Neither group had expected this. An awkward silence followed.

"Sou! Shouma!" Alka roared. "Your fate is now sealed! Whatever you and Eug are up to, it ends—!"

"Offal stew for two," Sou ordered, ignoring her entirely.

"What? Wait," Alka spluttered, but Sou just finished placing his order.

Only then did he turn to her. "We haven't spoken at length in some time," he intoned.

"At length, is it? You planning to repent your past misdeeds? You think I'll let you off the hook now?"

"Heavens, no," Sou said in exactly the same tone he'd used to order food. "The gears are already in motion. Nothing can stop them now—and I thought a warning would be fair."

"You certainly don't lack for confidence."

"Confidence is vital to deeds like—"

"Sir, your offal stew! Enjoy it while it's hot!"

The food came shockingly fast. Sou did as he was told and started eating immediately.

"*Mmph*...well, as a runeman...*huff*...I am unable to even die. Guilt itself is...*chomp*...unavoidable, yet— My word, the texture on this offal is marvelous!"

"Stop trying to enjoy stew and deliver a dramatic speech at the same time!"

"*Burp...* Have to eat it hot! My point is, I am part of the legend of the ancient heroes, so the only way I can vanish is if there is a modern-day hero. One admired far and wide. A sensation that delights one and all."

"And you're seriously trying to prop Lloyd up as this hero? The movies are just one step, all part of your efforts to advance society?"

Shouma jumped in, motormouthed, unable to sit by any longer. "Prop him up? Come now, Chief! We're giving him the boost he needs! Passionate twists! Passionate battles with demon lords! I just want that kid to experience all the satisfaction and fulfillment he could ever want! A goal, I might add, that is far less dubious than your habit of treating him like a dress-up doll."

"How dare you! I have never! He *enjoys* being my dress-up doll! I think!"

Ever heard of how people who are too similar never get along? This was exactly one of those situations.

As Sou watched their futile argument dispassionately, Marie spoke up.

"The ancient hero," she identified. "The man who saved the world."

"Yes."

"However heroic you once were, those of us from Azami will not easily forgive your actions since."

"Nor should you. I am now the villain the new hero must defeat. And that is how things must be if I am to disappear."

This could well be taken as sour grapes. It pushed Marie right through anger into disgust.

"You're putting the world in peril. Doesn't that take its toll on your heart?"

"I lost my heart a long time ago. However…"

But before Sou could say more, Shouma grabbed his shoulder. "Run for it, Sou! I pushed the chief too far!"

"I'm not a washboaaaaard!" Alka's fist shook, a sinister aura writhing behind her.

Sou rose to his feet, scratching his head. "Most unfortunate," he mumbled. "However long Alka lives, she remains physically undeveloped, a future bleak enough to make anyone give in to despair."

"This situation did not demand impromptu exposition!" Alka roared.

Sou swiftly dropped payment on the table and fled with Shouma.

"Wait, we're not done—," Marie called. They paid no heed.

"The past decade or so, I have felt tinges of emotion once again," Sou murmured. "Perhaps there are still those who desire my legend. Most unfortunate. We must eliminate them if I am to succeed in my goals."

"Quit muttering and move!" Shouma yelled. "The chief may be unstable, but she can still catch us if we don't book it!"

"Come back here! I demand recriminations! Reparations! And then your heads!"

Abandoning Marie entirely, the three raced off into the moonlit streets of Rokujou.

Meanwhile, back at the cadets' lodgings…the girls were repenting their failures at the audition in a lounge with a bay window view of the ocean.

"Thanks to Micona going berserk, that sure was a complete disaster," Selen said. "You're supposed to be the mature one here! Have you no sense at all?"

"You're one to talk," Riho muttered. Just who was it that spent all her time stalking Lloyd?

Meanwhile, Micona argued the point—rather sensibly.

"Then tell me, Selen Hemein. We all know you dote on Lloyd Belladonna. If you discovered some cabaret girl taking him for a ride, would you not try to kill her? Of course you would."

"Argh...you've got me there!" Selen wailed.

"Nah, killing really ain't the answer." Riho sighed.

Allan would normally go after Selen for something like this, but...

"...I'm a hopeless failure."

His disastrous audition had left him a miserable heap of self-pity. Without any external prompts whatsoever, he kept saying things like "I'm a failure," "Help," or "Sorry I was ever born." Anyone would get like that after giving a performance to rival any text-to-speech system, or maybe one of those cheap automated translators in a sci-fi film. And doing so right after arrogantly giving someone else acting tips.

The only person attempting to help Allan through yet another dark place on his life was Phyllo.

"......Mm," she said, putting a hand on his shoulder.

"I know! You're right, Phyllo. The only thing they want from cadets is action! It doesn't matter if we get any lines! You really make an excellent point."

"......I didn't say any of that." Phyllo frowned, regretting getting involved.

Riho sprawled back on the couch. "Allan ain't wrong, though. Auditioning extras ain't gonna get us cast as anything bigger than Passerby 1 in the end credits. They're looking for types, not talent."

"Exactly right! And Amidine was there, star of *Rokujou Holiday*! I'm sure he spotted Sir Lloyd and my potential immediately! We'll be cast as a couple, our passion captured on-screen! Cameras rolling all through our wedding night, capturing the action for eternity!"

How any acting talent could be spotted amid the chaos of the day was a mystery.

The mention of their wedding night left Riho beet-red. "You want them filming *that*?! That's just porn!"

Deadpan, Phyllo raised both hands, beckoning as if to say *Bring it on*.

"……I don't even *need* them filming," she said.

"Your friends are exhausting, Riho Flavin," Micona offered sympathetically. "I don't envy you."

"You're the last person I want sympathy from…" Riho sighed.

Micona had caused more problems than anyone else today. But at this point, she noticed a conspicuous absence.

"So where is Lloyd Belladonna anyway?"

"Excellent question!" Allan exclaimed, sitting up. "I didn't see him at the audition, either."

Just as they mentioned his name, Lloyd returned. Back in his usual form—an adorable boy with a gentle smile.

"Hey, everyone, sorry I'm so late."

"'Sup, Lloyd. What kept you?"

"Uh, kind of a long story. Had trouble tracking the chief down…"

"Welcome back, Lloyd," Allan said, bowing low. "I missed you at the audition hall. How fared your performance?"

"Uh, I think I kinda blew it. Still, no point crying about it now."

"Oh! I'd expect no less from you!"

"But your advice was really helpful, Allan."

"Mm? When did I give you any?"

"Whoops," Lloyd muttered and quickly tried to cover his mistake. "Er, uh…y-you forgot?"

"Huh…did I? I don't remember…"

If it came out that Lloyd was Roy, Micona might well go berserk again, so Riho and Selen hastily stepped in to help.

"Y-yo, Allan, you totally gave him tons of tips! Right, M'lady Selen?"

"He did! Very specific advice, like a veteran actor!"

Allan was starting to feel like maybe he *had* given Lloyd some help. He's definitely the type who gets easily hypnotized.

"R-right, now that you mention it! Sorry, I guess I did. Oh, that reminds me, I ran into this dude at the audition named Roy. Such a nice guy! He seemed familiar, but…"

Before Allan could finish the thought, Choline staggered in, looking exhausted.

"Kids! It's almost lights-out!"

She plopped herself down on the couch, appearing ready to go straight to sleep right there.

"You look really bushed, Colonel Choline. I thought you were relaxing at the inn while we auditioned?"

"No such luck, Riho!" Choline wailed. "I was on standby, stressing out the whole time! When the hell are they gonna make contact anyway?"

"Contact?"

Choline winced and hastily tried to cover her mistake. "Y-yeah. I mean, Amidine spoke to me earlier, right? Surely he'll be back to offer me a lead role!"

"Ever the optimist," Micona growled.

Wiping the sweat from her brow, Choline stuck out her tongue, saying, "Soooorry."

"I'm afraid that will not be happening, Colonel Choline," Selen declared. "The director has already chosen his lead actress."

"O-oh? Well, can't compete with the director's muse. Shame!"

But even off the hook, Choline just looked worn out. She sighed.

"Anyway, back to your rooms. I'll be going to bed myself soon. Ugh, if only Mena was here, too… Solo standby is grueling… *Zzz.*"

She fell asleep.

"Solo standby? What, did she need someone to play cards with her?"

"She mentioned 'contact.' I bet Colonel Choline's hiding something again…" Riho definitely got a whiff of something major going on here.

"She'll catch a cold sleeping here," Lloyd fussed. "We'd better take her to her room."

Little did he know the contact Choline had been waiting for had come to Lloyd—in his grown-up form.

"…Mm," Phyllo said, hefting Choline over her shoulder. She, too, was more deeply involved in this incident than she could possibly know. "…I'll drop her off…then join you in your bed, Master."

"Not happening!" Selen snapped. "Sir Lloyd lies with me!"

"Do you all wanna spend the night in a hotel or the slammer?"

"……If Master's with me, I could go either way."

Ignorance was bliss. Let's leave it at that.

In the depths of Rokujou's shopping district…a woman was gazing up at the night sky in a secluded corner.

Her pale skin reflected the moonlight, taking on an unearthly pallor. She spoke not a word, but then—her eyes shifted, looking to one side.

"……"

A girl with narrow eyes had appeared, out of breath—Mena.

"Hahh…hahh…I finally tracked you down!"

It was rare to see Mena look this intense. Her eyes met the moonlit woman's.

"…Go home," the woman growled and vanished into the darkness of the night.

"Wait! Come back!" Mena called, giving chase, but she'd already run herself ragged. It didn't take long before she tripped and fell.

When she staggered back to her feet, there was no sign of the woman.

"Why would you run from me…Mom?"

"I refuse to live a life where anyone else is using me."

One young man had made that his life's motto: Amidine Oxo.

He'd been a street urchin, growing up picking pockets and stealing what he could.

"If I want something, I take it, no matter what it is, no matter what I've gotta do."

Fueled by greed, he never thought twice about joining the Rokujou mob, becoming a part of the Rising Blue Dragon.

What waited for him there...was shabby treatment. He was an errand boy. Cannon fodder.

Only those with learning were allowed to run any part of the syndicate. The bosses and big shots earned those roles not through skill in a fight, but from higher education.

He wanted to prove himself—but the only jobs available to him were little better than the petty theft he'd grown up on. He constantly faced the humiliation of being a have-not.

But then...an aging gentleman and a tanned boy had appeared.

The gentleman seemed like the kind of battle-scarred veteran crime lord you could rely on, and Amidine didn't hesitate to vent his frustrations.

"I want it all. Power and fame to rival these damn intellectuals."

"Then join us," the tanned boy offered. "We can put you in charge, no prob."

"In exchange," the old man said, "when you control the mob, we want you developing cutting-edge weaponry—and your help making movies popular the world over. With our assistance, naturally."

"Why not become the lead actor yourself? There's your fame! Passion! We'll supply all the movie equipment."

Offered a way out of his predicament, Amidine leaped at the chance.

With their help, Amidine was soon a made man in the Rising Blue Dragon. And by his own talent, he'd claimed the boss's seat.

Hiding that fact from the world, he began producing films with himself as the star. His natural good looks proved very popular, and he was now the first person anyone in Rokujou thought of when they heard the words *movie star*. In return for this fame, he helped the gentleman and boy with their requests, using his star status to leverage politicians to their side.

The Rising Blue Dragon did whatever they had to, growing stronger and stronger, making themselves a central part of the government. Amidine was in charge and world-famous. He had everything he'd wanted—except for one thing.

"I'm just their errand boy!"

The cravings within never left him. The twisted drive that fueled him never let him go.

"If I had their wealth and resources, their knowledge... Perhaps I would at last be fulfilled."

The technology they offered was far beyond what anyone else had. And their fortune... If he could just make it all his, then—

"I'll be fulfilled. I'm done being used..."

It was time he used *them*. To do that, he needed their unquestioning trust.

That was why he accepted their every order, no matter how unpleasant. That was what brought him to this day.

*   *   *

Amidine got out of bed feeling out of sorts.

Smoking his morning cigarette, he stared at himself in the mirror and spat, "Morning, asshole."

He was still living at someone else's beck and call.

"Bumping people off... No different from when I was a hired hit man."

Swearing, he put his swanky suit on.

Always did feel like this after a murder. Same as I did when I was at the bottom, treated like trash.

A beautiful room, top-tier tobacco, luxury like he'd never even dreamed of in those days, but the aching discontent within always gnawed at him.

I don't even know what they're after. Why is making movies so important they fund theaters in every country? Because they want to film Lloyd's heroics for everyone to see? Who the hell is Lloyd anyway?!

Their love for Lloyd was beyond the comprehension of any ordinary man.

His nerves on edge, Amidine angrily fixed his hair.

Doesn't matter. Wait and see. I'm gonna take it all from you someday.

This mantra straightened his heart like the comb did his hair.

There was a knock on the door.

"Come in!"

A member of the film crew entered—an employee of the Rising Blue Dragon.

"Good morning, Boss. Your carriage awaits."

"Call me by my name," Amidine snapped. "Whether we're in private or not. Switching it up will just make it more likely you slip up when it matters. Don't want that, do we?"

"S-sorry, Amidine... You came back late last night. Anything amiss?"

"I sent the man in question to the harbor. He's fish food now. Wait for me outside."

The underling bowed and left.

Amidine made sure his tie was perfect, then left his room.

In the carriage, he sat with his arms folded, his eyes closed, going over the events of the night before.

That man—Roy, was it? His face when he learned he'd been betrayed... He'll come back to haunt me someday.

When they reached the set, voices called out to him, greeting him happily.

His grim look of a moment before forgotten, he met them all with a pleasant smile, responding to every greeting.

Haunt me all you like. You can't get fame and revolutionary technology without a few sacrifices. Watch with envy as I make it all mine. But for now, the movie. No time to spend on idle thoughts.

He slapped himself lightly on the cheek, focusing his mind, totally committed to playing the movie star.

The cadets and soldiers from Azami were waiting, looking nervous. When they saw Amidine looking, they began politely greeting him.

"Good morning!"

In the crowd...was Lloyd—in his grown-up form.

"You're haunting me alreadyyyyyyyyyyyyyy?!" Amidine shrieked.

Lloyd looked confused. "Um, is something wrong?"

"What isn't?! It's just yesterday! Not even a full day! I know I was thinking you could haunt me if you wanted, but isn't this too soon?!"

"Haunt? Um, aren't we meeting now?" Lloyd in Roy form just blinked at him.

Amidine was getting increasingly confused.

Who is this guy?! I know for a fact I shot him through the heart and watched the harbor for an hour to make sure he didn't surface! No human can stay down that long!

Lloyd could, unfortunately. He's from Kunlun.

Amidine wasn't done yet.

And why is he here? He knows I'm the boss of the Rising Blue Dragon! I told him! And then I shot him through the heart! Why does he look happy to see me? Who would be? No, wait...

Amidine found an improbable explanation for an impossible situation.

Does he have amnesia? He lost so much blood he can't remember any of that? Of course! That explains it!

"Oh, Amidine, thanks for the acting tips last night."

"So you *do* remember?!"

His last shred of hope dissipated. But why was he calling it acting tips? Amidine clutched his spinning head.

What does that mean?! Why is he okay?! Didn't I shoot him?!

Then a light bulb went off over his head.

Oh! I see! Of course an agent from Azami would wear a bulletproof vest! And he knows full well Sardin would never believe I'm the boss of the Rising Blue Dragon without solid evidence! That's why he's playing dumb, seeing how I react! Looking for his shot at stealing back the pendant!

Amidine gave Lloyd an impressed look, having talked himself into admiring his opponent's gumption. Like the fabled duel between a conniving fox and a cunning tanuki. Like a consort playing innocent and a regular john. Like Hajime Kindaichi, alleged grandson of a great detective, and the culprit. Suddenly trapped in a battle of wits, Amidine kicked his mind into high gear.

All of this showed on his face—a far cry from his usual confident charm—and that attracted Sardin's attention.

"Something ailing you, Amidine?"

"N-not at all, Your Majesty."

"Well, if you say so!" Sardin's faith in him was clearly unwavering.

Now Amidine just had to do something about Lloyd.

If he gets the pendant back from me and uses it to free Ubi, then we lose our trump card and can no longer force Sardin to keep Rokujou under our thumb. Worse—if Sardin finds out I have the pendant, I'm blown!

The pendant was in his pocket right now—a pendant Amidine had no business holding on to. This could be decisive evidence. If he was seen with it, the king would know instantly who he was. He was in trouble, like a killer concealing the bloodstained murder weapon.

Just as Amidine was starting to panic, he spotted two men watching the set in the distance.

Th-the sponsors! They came to watch us filming?

They were on the balcony of a café overlooking the location. Another light bulb went off, this one even bigger.

Yes! I could ask them to kill Roy for me! They should be up to the task! And they don't want anything disrupting the movie business, either!

Amidine raced over to the café to talk to them.

"Hmm, I don't see Lloyd anywhere… What a shame."

"I heard the cadets from Azami were here and came running, but… hmm."

Sou and Shouma were elegantly sipping tea, searching for Lloyd.

Then Amidine came rushing over, out of breath.

"Yo, Amidine," Shouma greeted, blinking at him. "What's up? Jogging to shed a few pounds? Passion!"

"Please!" Amidine begged, bowing low. "I need your help!"

Sou and Shouma glanced at each other, taken aback.

"Hmm, perhaps start with some water," Sou said, pouring him a glass.

Amidine chugged it and then began to explain the situation.

All about Sardin's plan to bring in Azami soldiers as backup. How Amidine had failed to off their main agent…and how that could disrupt the entire movie enterprise.

He switched between acknowledging his own failings and offering apologies between explanations.

Sou and Shouma listened gravely.

"If we don't do something, it could all go under. But with your help… You don't need to kill him. You could lock him up somewhere or…or even just get him kicked out of the military!"

Sou offered absolutely nothing.

Looking increasingly desperate, Amidine admitted, "I know, killing people is my job. But if I make the wrong move here, my cover's blown. They'll know I'm with the mob."

"Listen. This is very important," Shouma said. "Was one of the Azami cadets named Lloyd? Cute kid, chestnut hair?"

"Er, no…I've read all the paperwork, and there was nobody named Lloyd."

Amidine blinked at him, rattled by the question. Paying this no heed…

"Then let's send them packing!" Shouma cried.

"Mm."

They readily agreed to the task at hand.

What does Lloyd have to do with anything?!

Amidine kept a smile plastered on his face, disguising the screaming inside. "Thank you," he said, bowing his head low.

"Developing the world is vital," Sou added. "If they would interfere with that, they are not welcome here."

Amidine relaxed at last.

Then Shouma asked, "So who was it that didn't die when you shot them? Selen? Her belt, Vritra, might be able to pull off a trick like that, but we can't kill her! She's Lloyd's friend."

The wind back in his sails, Amidine pointed to the man who refused to die—Roy Akizuki, aka Lloyd Belladonna.

"That boy there. Roy Akizuki."

""………"" They both froze instantly.

"Um? Hello? Is something wrong?"

Neither seemed to hear Amidine's question. They were both staring fixedly at the young man under discussion.

"What do you make of it, Shouma?"

"That's definitely Lloyd. The way he's keeping that piece of candy in his cheek, the way he shifts his weight from side to side, the way he's fussing with his hair—all Lloyd things."

These two Lloyd addicts had seen through his disguise instantly. Shouma was being downright creepy.

"Has his current form…been caused by one of Alka's runes?"

"I bet the chief just wanted to dress him up and convinced him extras need to be tall or something. And Akizuki… Isn't that her old name?"

"Ruka Akizuki, I believe. Eug got all clever with it and turned that into Aruka, then Alka."

Amidine was feeling entirely left out now, not understanding a word of this. He elected to listen in silence. *Who are these people? I'd kill 'em in a second if it weren't for their money and technology…*

A moment later, they both turned toward him.

"Are you done now?" Amidine asked. "Then please, eliminate this—"

"Don't be ridiculous," Shouma snapped. "We'd never do that."

"Huh?"

"Sponsors demand that you put Roy Akizuki in a lead role."

"Huh? Uh, wait, but I'm the lead…"

"Then drop out. Become an extra. Give him the help he needs."

Amidine turned to Sou for help.

"This is mandatory, Amidine. If you refuse, we'll withdraw all financial and technological support and expose all misdeeds the Rising Blue Dragon have ever committed. Everyone will know you're a mob boss. And you don't want that, do you?"

Amidine felt like the world was crashing down. He gasped for air.

Sou merely glared at him like a judge who'd just passed a sentence. Amidine knew better than to argue with that look. Heedless of what Amidine was asking for, they both had that look of smug satisfaction people get after scoring a good deal on a household appliance.

"So go on, sort it out! This is such a passionate twist, Sou!"

"Indeed it is! We can capture Lloyd's bravery on film, edit it, and have all the propaganda we need for the days to come."

"Man, adult Lloyd sure is a looker. His boy form ain't bad, but this has a flair all its own. Definitely heroic-looking!"

"Quite heroic, yes."

But their Lloyd talk fell on deaf ears.

"Argh…it doesn't matter what I want, huh?" Amidine growled. "I… have to drop out? Become an extra…?"

If he insisted on playing the lead, his career would be forcibly ended. As he gritted his teeth, Amidine felt his knees wobbling.

Meanwhile, grown-up Lloyd—Roy—and the girls were in nearby tents, getting their makeup done and getting fitted for their costumes.

They were being dressed as a passerby, a waitress, a street vendor, and the like.

"Uh, no costume for me?" Riho asked.

"Sorry, dear," the costumer said. "You were supposed to be a passerby, but we didn't have any clothes that could hide that arm."

She glanced down at the bulky lump of mithril covering Riho's left arm.

"No prob," Riho said, waving it off.

"You're sure, Riho?" Lloyd asked. "You won't be in the movie!"

"Nah, I got bigger fish to fry." Riho grinned. "I mean, that's *too bad*! I *really* wanted to be in this movie!"

"You're so obvious," Selen said, rolling her eyes.

Riho had always been planning on swiping the lead actor's used chopsticks, so this worked out just fine.

She turned to leave, sticking her tongue out. "Such a shaaaame!" she continued. "I guess I'll just have to go scope out the vicinity around Amidine…"

Phyllo's hand clamped down on her shoulder.

"Ow! What the heck, Phyllo?"

"…Anyone not cast is part of the crew. That's the rule."

"Crew… You mean, we're working for *free*?"

Her chance at a fortune had abruptly turned into a volunteer opportunity. Riho was visibly annoyed.

"It's not *free*. They're paying for our lodgings, after all. And we get to make memories with Sir Lloyd…!" Then Selen smirked and put a hand over her mouth. "But I guess if you're part of the crew, you can only watch us having fun from the sidelines."

"...You poor thing." Phyllo started fake crying.

Riho's brow twitched. She opened her mouth to snarl something back...but a low, sad voice called out to her.

"Heyyy...over heeeere..."

"Is somebody crying? Ugh!"

Riho had turned to find Allan and a group of very gloomy cadets hauling equipment around.

"Don't look so peeved, mercenary. You're like us! Part of the *crew*."

Allan managed a feeble laugh, cradling a bounce board—the white thing they use to reflect light during a shoot—like it was a valuable treasure.

"You can't have a movie...*sob*...without a crew."

"We're part of things! Still!"

"*Hic...* Where there's light, there's shadow. And we...matter, too."

The rest of the cadets started beckoning to Riho, sinister smiles on their lips. They were all pretty bad actors... The last one hadn't even worked on his line in advance and had paused for an awfully long time before awkwardly wrapping things up.

"They all thought they'd be in the movie but failed miserably! They were stamped with the 'disqualified extra' brand and plunged into darkness," Selen intoned.

"And...I gotta be one of them?" Riho asked, looking aghast.

Phyllo gave her a comforting pat on the shoulders. "...Don't let the darkness swallow you," she advised.

"I won't! Dammit! This isn't fair! I gotta work for free *and* get lumped in with these losers?!"

But Riho's desperate wail vanished futilely into the skies of Rokujou.

Then someone seeming even more desperate appeared—Amidine— looking like he'd dropped both his wallet *and* his keys.

Everyone turned to stare, wondering what had happened.

Then Sardin appeared, holding a megaphone in one hand—as movie directors are wont to do.

"Well, now that Amidine's arrived, let's all get to know one another! What's that you say? 'You're famous, King Sardin. We need no introduction'? Well, where's the fun in *that*?"

He spoke with the enthusiasm of a lonely guy hosting his first and only singles party. Nervous laughter went up all over.

A vein twitched on Amidine's forehead. He moved closer.

"Wh-what's wrong Amidine? You look unwell…huh?"

"Uh, so," Amidine whispered in Sardin's ear, eyes hollow. "The sponsors want to cast Mr. Akizuki as the lead."

Sardin's eyes went wide, rattled. "B-but…," he protested, low and furious. "We wanted him slipping away from filming to investigate the mob's activities! Dammit, the Rising Blue Dragon are definitely behind this…"

"No, this is entirely unrelated to them," Amidine said. "I swear."

"Er… How are you so sure?"

He was the boss of the Rising Blue Dragon, after all.

Sardin put a hand to his brow, then sighed and snapped back into his Dumb Dandy act.

"Sorry for the delay, everyone! I actually have a surprise casting announcement! Is everyone ready? No, perhaps that's the wrong tone to strike…"

Recasting the lead role really wasn't news to deliver like a hype man. You wouldn't want a baseball coach going, "Woohoo! You just got demoted to the bench!"

Seeing Sardin at a loss, Amidine listlessly explained, "Sorry to spring this on everyone, but I've been forced to drop out."

Everyone gulped.

"B-but—who else can play the lead?!" Lloyd fretted.

Looking like he'd lost his own soul, Amidine patted him on the shoulder.

"You will, Mr. Akizuki."

"""""Whaaaaaaaaaaaaaaaaaaat?!"""""

Lloyd was not the only one astonished by this announcement.

"Wait... What the heck?" Riho said, baffled.

"Isn't it obvious?" Selen asked, looking very proud. "They spotted Sir Lloyd's unmissable talent. My very own star!"

"He ain't yours, and his audition was canceled!" Riho snapped. She gave Amidine a suspicious look...and saw tears running down his face. "Why's he crying?"

"Moved to tears by the birth of the hero of the new age!"

Really? Riho gave him a long, searching look.

"Goddamn sponsors," he muttered, shaking with rage.

"He seems to be blaming the sponsors..."

"The sponsors' eyes must have lit upon Sir Lloyd and seen the aura of greatness shining off him! Poor Amidine couldn't even compete!"

That wasn't what she'd said a moment ago, and Riho was about to point this out but decided against it. "Well, showbiz is complicated," she said, chalking it up to grown-up problems. But the grown-ups causing this were doing so for extremely childish reasons...

"Anyway, Roy! I'm sure we all—*all*—have opinions on this, but as our new lead actor, can you say a word or two to everyone?"

Rather flustered by all of this, Lloyd looked around at the cast and crew.

"Er, um...I'm as confused as everyone, but I'll do my best!"

Yeah, in a situation like this, that was definitely the safe thing to say.

Amidine's cheeks were stained with tears. Lloyd was at a total loss. Sardin's usual bluster wasn't really concealing his dismay—and the cast were forced to applaud all three of them. But no one really felt like celebrating, so the applause was not exactly thunderous.

The room had that awkward vibe of a going-away party for a boss who's been let go.

The other cast members stepped up, introducing themselves—a fierce-looking villain, a hard-boiled veteran cop, and a beautiful village girl.

All were surprised by the sudden recasting, but they each said nice things: "This happens in the biz!" or "Break a leg!"

And as they introduced themselves…

"……" One girl seemed distinctly out of place. She had a parasol raised, hiding her face.

Spying this, Sardin turned everyone's attention to her.

"And this is our heroine! Mina will be playing a girl who flees the palace! Be nice to her, everyone! …Say hi, Mina."

With that, Mina closed her parasol and bowed.

"……Um, I'm Mina. Nice to meet you."

She had blond hair past her shoulders. She wore a blue hat and a lovely dress. Her big round eyes made quite an impression. She didn't raise her voice and kept her greeting simple.

The crowd was somewhat nonplussed by this.

"Uh, she's a little nervous!" Sardin explained. "This is her first big role! And obviously, she wants to avoid getting burned by the sun."

Riho narrowed her eyes. "He's sure got her back… Oh, is she the one he personally cast?"

She'd heard something about him insisting they cast unknown talent in the role.

"King Sardin plucked her out of obscurity! Now she and Sir Lloyd… Oh, I'm so jealous." Selen chewed on a fingernail, scowling at Mina furiously, as if she was convinced she should be the one up there on that stage.

Relieved he wasn't the only one with his first big role, Lloyd came up to Mina, smiling gently.

"I—I guess we're both beginners, then?" he said. "This won't be easy, but if we work together, I'm sure we can— Hmm?"

Mina had stepped behind him, standing very close and pulling her hat down low over her eyes. A bead of sweat ran down her cheek.

It was like she was hiding from Lloyd's friends. He heard her whisper, "Oh, crap."

Lloyd looked confused.

"…Mm?" Phyllo's eyes had gone wide, staring fixedly at Mina.

"Oh, already in character, Mina?" Sardin cried.

"…Who does she think she is?" Selen's eyes were equally wide.

"I've been biding my time…but that home-visiting escort has already seduced another victim!"

Micona was doing the exact same thing—except she was here "biding her time" to bump off grown-up Lloyd. She was radiating murder.

"She's probably just scared because the three of you are glaring at her…although she is standing a bit *too* close to him." Riho's eyes narrowed.

With boundless good cheer, Sardin urged the girls to leave.

"Now the Azami contingent will be filming a scene in the shopping district, so please head on over there! Roy, let me get you the script."

"Boo…" Selen was visibly displeased, clearly wanting to stay by Lloyd's side.

"I know you want to watch me work," Sardin said. "But I'll catch up with you all at the next location."

"No, not you, Sardin! Sir Ll—"

Riho stepped in, clapping a hand over Selen's mouth.

"That's enough out of you, m'lady. Better secure the girl behind you on the right."

Selen looked over her right shoulder…and found Micona repeating, "Guilty as charged, guilty-guilty-guilty…" without pausing for breath, like a *kabaddi* player chanting throughout her game.

"It would never do to have her cause another scene like yesterday, I suppose."

"Yo, Phyllo, don't just stand there! Let's move!"

"……Mm." Phyllo finally blinked and reluctantly joined them.

Once they were gone, Lloyd heard Mina breathe a sigh of relief.

"Thought my cover was blown for sure," she muttered.

"Huh?"

"Oh, nothing," she said, waving him off.

Lloyd looked puzzled, but someone was calling out to him. "Roy Akizuki! We've got a scene to film, so change into the lead's costume and head to that warehouse."

"Oh, right! Thanks! Uh…Mina?"

She was still in his shadow, but hastily emerged. "Oh…sorry…Roy."

"Not a problem, Mina. If you'll excuse me."

He bowed and ran off back to makeup.

"…Since when did the Azami army have a hunk like that?" she muttered, but this…Lloyd did not hear.

Now then, what happened to Amidine, reduced to being an extra?

As he stood there with the empty eyes of one who's lost everything, a Rising Blue Dragon member slipped up to him, mingling with the crew.

"Bo—Amidine, what's going on? Why would you give up the lead role?"

Amidine didn't even have the energy to scold the man for almost calling him Boss.

"The sponsors insisted," he explained, smiling slightly. "If I don't agree, not only will they cut off our weapons supply, they'll expose us all."

"S-seriously?"

"Seriously. If it weren't for him… If only…yes."

An idea came to Amidine.

"Let's get rid of Mr. Akizuki. That way I can get the lead role back and crush Sardin's plans. Gather every underling you can."

"Y-yes, sir!"

Life back in his eyes, Amidine grinned and let out an ominous chuckle.

The warehouse on the outskirts of Rokujou was normally used to store bricks, lumber, and other building supplies, but today, it was filled with actors and equipment.

Lloyd changed into the costume the stylist provided, looking bashful.

Black slacks and jacket over a green shirt and a red necktie—not at all the sort of clothes he was used to wearing, and he felt very uncomfortable in them.

The stylist noticed that at once. "It's perfect," she assured. "If your girlfriend sees this, she'll swoon."

Lloyd had actually sent five girls into a swan dive the other day, except none of them were his girlfriend.

"O-oh, I don't have a—" Lloyd turned red. This look on the face of a twentysomething hunk was definitely a surprise, and one that clearly worked for the stylist.

Then a man came up and introduced himself as the screenwriter. He had...very dead eyes.

"So you're Roy, huh? The one taking over for Amidine?"

"A-are you okay?"

"I'm doing better than the AD...and the PAs looked ready to die from ulcers. Lord knows how many retakes or revisions this'll require." He handed Lloyd a copy of the script. "There's a number of changes to fit the new casting, so take a look."

"Okay, sure. Thank you."

Seeing Lloyd's nervous expression, the screenwriter gave him an encouraging look.

"This is the sponsors' fault, not yours. And motion pictures don't have any sound, so nobody'll notice if your lines are a bit off. Most times we can fix it in the captions. Later!"

He turned and left, and Lloyd let out a sigh of relief.

"It's good to be more composed," Mina comforted, but then she twisted the knife. "But it's harder than it sounds. If you start babbling nonsense, the other actors'll get rattled, and if that shows on their faces... Just make sure you're prepared."

"Uh, good point, Mina."

"The key is improvising."

This actually put a little confidence on Lloyd's face.

"Oh! So that's why King Sardin and Amidine ran me through that yesterday... Okay, I just have to do it like that! Like they're really trying to kill me."

Yeah, that wasn't acting. He really was trying to kill you.

Just then... *Yoink.*

"Huh?"

At the mention of their names, Mina grabbed Lloyd, pulling him in close.

"King Sardin? And Amidine? What did you do with them? They tried to kill you?"

Lloyd blinked at her, very surprised by the steely glint in her eyes.

"Er, yes... After the audition..."

"Yo, Mr. Akizuki! How are you feeling? I feel great myself, like a dog out for a walk!"

Before Lloyd could say another word about the day before, Sardin cut in, extra enthusiastic.

"Your Majesty... No, you're the director now, right? Looking forward to working with you, sir. Sorry, this must be a big mess."

Lloyd bowed low. Sardin bobbed his head right back.

"I'm the one who's sorry! Springing all this on you—but you can't argue with the moneymen. They're providing all this equipment! I know I'm asking a lot of you, but just act natural, and our top-tier crew will make this a movie to remember! Relax!"

Then he leaned in, whispering in Lloyd's ear—suddenly very serious.

"Oh, and...mister, I know Mina's cute, but don't tell her about yesterday. You never know who's watching. Make sure to act natural where that's concerned, too."

He had no idea Lloyd had mistaken that for an improv—nobody would. He was just taking precautions to make extra sure Lloyd's lips were sealed.

I can see why he wants me keeping quiet. They can't tell anyone about secret auditions. But...who could be watching?

Since he assumed everything yesterday had been part of his audition, Lloyd was confused by this ominous turn of phrase.

Sensing this, Sardin leaned even closer. Too close. Lloyd could feel the man's breath on his cheek.

"What's this? You don't think Mina's cute?"

"Er, no, that isn't…"

"At any rate, not a word to anyone. No matter how cute Mina is, we can't get her involved in this."

Lloyd assumed this was Sardin's way of saying he couldn't have his own actress get caught up in a scandal. He was rather at a loss.

"Director, you've left him nowhere to go. Maybe cut the kid a break?" Mina suggested.

"Mm! But of course! I was just about to do that!"

With a blissful smile, he shot her a thumbs-up. This…was not part of his Dumb Dandy routine. One hundred percent his natural reaction.

How deep does Mina have her claws in him? wondered the entire crew.

Then the assistant director appeared, looking ready to cry. The sudden recasting had played havoc with the entire shoot schedule…and she was fighting the urge to just run for the hills.

"Who raised you people? The cameras are over there! You need to be on set! You're the director!"

"*Gasp!* Right you are! My parents would be ashamed of me!"

"Stop posing, you Dumb Dandy! Just get a move on!"

"Of course, right away! Mister, I trust you completely, but don't you lay a finger on Mina or—"

Sardin was dragged away across the warehouse floor. So much for regal dignity.

Lloyd was still stuck on the line about not knowing who's watching.

Oh! He must mean the cameras. They must have cameras hidden everywhere so they can capture behind-the-scenes footage!

This sort of footage was often played during the end credits—along with bloopers and unused scenes.

With this entirely wrong idea in mind, Lloyd braced himself. *I can't let my guard down at all!* he thought. This wasn't a variety show, though, so if they wanted footage from the set, nobody would resort to spy tactics.

Lloyd immediately started acting highly suspicious, and Mina raised an eyebrow at him.

"You tight with the king?" she asked.

"I wouldn't say that...I mean, you seem much closer to him than I am."

"Not really. He doesn't talk about himself much, and the whole Dumb Dandy thing is just an act. I oughtta know."

"Really? As an actor yourself?"

"And it's less that we're close than he's carrying a one-sided torch for me. I dunno what his deal is or what he's really thinking...or why he's teamed up with Amidine. Sorry, I'm getting sidetracked." Mina broke off, settling down on the step of a nearby ladder. "Either way, the sponsors like you...so your fate is sealed. Try not to embarrass the army of Azami, okay? If this winds up souring relations with Rokujou, Choline will be pissed."

"Colonel Choline? You know her?"

"Whoops! Yeah, well, she's from Rokujou, you know! She's a famous recovery magic expert! Also, uh, you know how to read scripts and everything? I'll give you a free lesson! Ask your wallet and your legal guardians if you can afford that low, low fee!"

Her entire manner changed. It struck Lloyd as familiar somehow. But he jumped on the offer.

"Please!"

"The key is to not overthink things," Mina began.

Amidine and his main crew-member henchman were watching from behind a bookcase, like classroom outcasts cursing the popular kids.

What they actually said was even more ominous.

"Ready to send him to the great beyond?"

"Yes, sir. Exactly as ordered. See?" The underling glanced toward a simple steel-pipe scaffolding. There were lights and other heavy objects piled on top.

Sturdy bolts held the whole thing together, but someone was busy loosening those. Another Rising Blue Dragon minion.

With the bolts loosened, it would only take a nudge to send the whole thing crashing down. Amidine flashed a toothy grin. "Heh-heh-heh... well done. The moment he steps beneath it..."

All that heavy gear would come crashing down on Lloyd's head. A classic murder technique: making it look like an accident.

"But Bo—Amidine, won't this take Mina out, too?"

The underling seemed far less enthused by this plan.

"Watch what you call me," Amidine scolded, poking him. "The life of an up-and-coming young actress versus the survival of the Rising Blue Dragon? You don't have to be a brainiac to answer that question. Don't miss your chance to rub Roy out."

"S-sorry."

Without a second glance at his minion, Amidine chuckled—all trace of his dashing movie star act long since gone.

"Heh-heh-heh... You can't put a bulletproof vest on your head! Enjoy having your skull caved in."

This was downright disturbing, and his minion visibly flinched.

Mina waved Lloyd over, and he stepped closer. Amidine's eyes flashed.

"Now! Do it!"

Catching the signal, the minion near the scaffolding gave the loosened bolt a kick.

Clang! Clatter! The iron scaffolding went flying—

"......Huh?"

"Mina, look out!"

Equipment and scaffolding alike came crashing mercilessly down on their heads.

Shrieks went up from the crew nearby. The sounds of steel rods clanging and heavy objects landing echoed, and a cloud of dust went up...

"Got him!" Behind the shelf, Amidine pumped a fist, certain the collapse had found its mark.

"Yes, definitely." His minion shuddered. "I saw a steel pipe hit that Roy fellow right in the head…"

"His skull's caved in! His neck's fractured! No way he survived that," Amidine cried jubilantly, watching for the dust cloud to settle.

He was like a young boy pulling on a *gacha* game, waiting for the rainbow sparkles to dissipate, not daring to blink.

When the dust cleared, Amidine saw…

"Are you okay, Mina?"

Lloyd was completely uninjured. Mina was cradled in his arms like he was carrying a princess.

"You're kidding! You said you saw a pipe bounce right off his head!"

"I—I know I did! It hit him so hard, it flattened the pipe!"

"Then how is he not dead?!"

Amidine and his minion weren't getting anywhere hiding behind that bookshelf.

Oblivious to their consternation, Lloyd aimed his gentle smile at Mina—with his much more handsome grown-up face.

"That was a surprise, huh? All that equipment falling like that."

The blow would have killed any mere mortal, so Mina was gaping up at him in surprise.

"Er, huh? How are you okay?"

Mina was well aware this was a stupid question, but she couldn't not ask.

"Well, I am a soldier!" he explained. "They train us pretty well. Something like this is no big deal."

No amount of training would allow anyone to survive that kind of blunt force trauma. But for someone from Kunlun, it really *wasn't* a big deal. The iron pipe bent to the shape of Lloyd's head proved that.

Mina stared up at Lloyd's smile for a bit, then realized she was stuck in his arms and turned bright red.

"W-w-whoa!" she cried, thrashing about.

Lloyd gently put her down. "Oh, sorry, was that weird?"

"Not exactly! It just…caught me by surprise! It's not every day you get snatched up in someone's arms! If I was a balloon, I'd have popped!"

Something about her flustered actions tugged at the back of Lloyd's mind like déjà vu. "Hmm," he said, cocking his head. "Sorry, uh...I feel like I've heard someone talk like you before..."

This made Mina even more flustered.

"Whoops, uh... More importantly, why did this thing collapse on... Mm?"

Her eyes locked on to something in the distance. There was a glint in them so powerful, Lloyd thought she was mad at him.

"Wh-what's wrong? Did I mess something up?"

"Mm? No, sorry, sorry, nothing. Huh...I feel like I've heard *that* before..."

Now it was Lloyd's turn to adopt a suspicious look. Mina quickly dismissed the idea, shaking it off.

By this point, the crew was running over, yelping at the pile of scaffolding and the fallen ladder.

"A-are you two okay? What happened?" someone called.

"We're fine!" Mina assured, smiling. "No injuries, thankfully."

The crew looked relieved. "Well, good...but why did the scaffolding collapse? Were the bolts left loose?"

"...Maybe," Mina muttered, glaring at the shadows behind the bookcase as the crew started the cleanup effort.

Behind the bookcase, the Rising Blue Dragon minion caught Mina's look.

"Bo...I mean, Amidine. I think that woman might be on to us. Might be better to lie low for a while."

Amidine was in no mood to pay his minion any heed. He was too preoccupied with Lloyd's ability to withstand damage.

"Who cares if some silly girl saw us?! Does that man have a steel cap under his scalp?!"

Even if he did, the impact of that blow would still crush one's spine.

Amidine was clearly in no state to realize the obvious. His minion shot him a look of pity.

"That wouldn't help, really...but that girl got herself cast in this film and has been sniffing around us. Weren't we on our guard around her? Mina must not her real name, either. Should we take care of her?"

"If we can't hurt him from the outside...we'll have to try *inside*."

"Er...what are we talking about? Amidine?"

Amidine quit muttering and wheeled around to face his minion.

"The first scene they're filming is the hero and heroine talking in a café, right?"

"Y-yeah."

"Then we poison him! Slip some poison in the coffee they're using. We have a powerful one back at the office, right? Go get it!"

"W-we do, but...using poison in a crowd like this? If it gets traced back to us..."

Before his minion could finish, Amidine grabbed a fistful of his shirt, snarling, "I said go get it now! Did you not hear me?"

Sweating profusely, the henchman nodded vigorously and then sprinted off toward the office. Amidine had maintained the dashing good-guy act for a long time, but now his eyes were hollow and empty, his shoulders shaking with a malevolent cackle.

"You steal my part...I'll kill you with the cameras rolling. I'll preserve your death for eternity!"

With his makeup perfect, Lloyd entered the café set for his first scene.

The camera and lights were all in position, and the air was buzzing with energy.

The camera looked like a bazooka with two mouse ears attached. Lloyd faced it, bracing himself.

"Relax," Mina urged. "It's not actually a bazooka. I know, it does sort of feel like facing a firing squad..."

"Uh, okay!" Lloyd exclaimed, turning back to her.

Mina chuckled. "You're funny," she said. "You look all grown up, but sometimes you react like a kid."

"Oh, uh…sorry?"

Mina looked almost as sheepish as he did. They took their seats before the camera lens.

"You've got your script? This is where the lead and heroine get to know each other. The heroine goes to the restroom and doesn't come back, and the lead fears she's been kidnapped and goes after her."

"Uh, right. I-I'll do my best!"

"Don't sweat it. You can fudge the lines a bit; I'll keep up."

"I-I'll do my best," Lloyd said again, sounding like a broken record.

"Oh? Oh?" Mina teased. "Not good at talking to cute girls, are you?"

"Huh? I would have said you're more beautiful than cute…"

Mina's eyes went wide, and she turned bright red. Ah, romance.

"Er, uh, sorry." Lloyd sure was apologizing a lot.

"Geez." Mina scolded him to cover her own embarrassment. "Keep it together. We've got a big action scene after this, and the producer will be there. Can't have you looking nervous there. I won't be in that scene, so good luck."

"Uh, right…the producer?"

Nobody had mentioned this role yet.

"They keep the movie moving. Every motion picture has one. If the director is like the father, the producer is the mother of the film."

Lloyd nodded as if it all made sense. "Okay, I get that! That would make you the older sister, then? A very reliable one, at that."

"I…suppose. Yeah, you can count on me as an older sister." There seemed to be some veiled meaning behind this. Mina leaned across the table. "You wouldn't have a little brother, would you? One of the cadets?"

"Nope. No brother."

"Yeah, your names are different… Anyway, you sure reacted quick. Almost like Phyllo…and you're really well-built."

This made Mina remember the feel of his arms around her. She blushed again.

"Something wrong?"

"N-nothing! W-we're filming soon, right? When do we start?"

Mina noticed the crew grinning at them and fanned her face, hoping the red would go away.

"Wish we'd had the camera rolling!" Sardin cried. "Mr. Akizuki, if we tell the tabloids how fast you went after your costar, I bet they'd pay top dollar! Ha-ha-ha!"

The crew took this as a joke and laughed, but Sardin's eyes showed no signs of mirth.

"Quit joking around and let's film this thing!" the assistant director hissed. "We're on a tight schedule, remember?"

"True, but Amidine isn't here yet."

"Oh?"

"Yeah, he said he wanted to be in this scene."

"I'm here now." Amidine swept in, dressed in an apron—playing the café owner.

"You're late! What kept you?"

"Had trouble getting the pois—*ahem*—the right apron."

Amidine gestured proudly at his apron, which featured adorable kitties. Everyone was shocked into silence. This was an awfully cute look for him… He'd actually been waiting for the poison to arrive.

Paying no heed to the horrified looks, he tugged the kitty-cat apron strings tight and clapped his hands.

"Let's start filming! I'll serve a cup of coffee to Mr. Akizuki, and he'll take a sip before saying his lines! Drink it up! Go on, drink away!"

"Uh…I guess you're in character, huh? Always a professional. Full bore even for a bit part."

Sardin grabbed his megaphone and started barking instructions.

"Let's do this! Roll camera! Scene fifteen! Action!"

At his order, a hum filled the room. The camera sprang to life. Mina began to speak, looking relaxed.

Lloyd's performance was slightly stilted, but well within the confines of the scene. As they went through their lines, Amidine arrived with their coffee.

"Your coffee. And the check."

"Thank you."

Amidine went back to the kitchen, watching Lloyd's lips like a hawk as the coffee was lifted toward them.

"Go on! Die! May your stomach melt!" he hissed.

The coffee touched Lloyd's lips...and he downed the cup.

"Now die! Go on...die...any minute now..."

The scene wrapped up.

"And cut! Good work, Roy! A fine performance for your first outing."

"Stop right there!" Amidine came storming out of the kitchen.

"What's wrong, Amidine? Was his performance unsatisfactory?"

"It was fine!"

"Er, it was?"

Then why had he come flying out of the kitchen?

"Mr. Akizuki!"

"Y-yes?"

"Did you...drink the coffee? Well? Say something!"

"Er... Yeah. It was a little on the sour side, but still good?"

"That's it?!"

Everyone was staring at him. And not in the way you'd look at a movie star. It was more like the look you'd direct at a crazy old man.

"Amidine, you're a bit too into this role. We're done filming, so no need to play the part of the coffee fanatic café owner any longer. Time to break character, mm?"

"Sour?! Just...sour?!" Amidine fell to his knees, weeping.

As he did, Mina's eyes caught a glimpse of something.

A plain-looking pendant.

"Is that the Saint's Pendant? Why does he have it?" Mina hissed under her breath, scowling at him. "I'll have to snatch it away from him... I've got to get my hands on it!"

*   *   *

"What the hell happened out there?! Didn't you bring me the shit I asked for?!" Amidine shrieked in a corner of the empty kitchen, holding a member of his organization up by the collar.

From a distance, he looked like a café owner scolding a part-timer... except he was making full use of his mafia-taught ways. Whatever happened to hiding his identity?

"I did! I promise!" squeaked the minion. Amidine eyed him dubiously. His kitty-cat apron was making this scene almost comical.

"Then why is he still alive? ...That wasn't what you said it would do! Don't tell me you brought me cold medicine—or worse, powdered sugar!"

In a huff, Amidine scraped the bottom of Lloyd's cup with his fingernail and brought it to his lips.

"It's sweet. Don't tell me you actually gave me— Gweh-gah-gah-gah-gah-gah!"

"Ah, Amidine! No! Spit it out! There you go! And rinse out your mouth with some water! Say 'aaah'!"

His subordinate sounded like he was scolding a child who'd eaten something he wasn't supposed to. He handed Amidine a glass of water.

"Yow! My tongue! Ow! ...*Glug-glug.* Bleh. *Glug-glug.* Bleh. *Glug-glug...*"

Pain finally subsided, Amidine slumped over in exhaustion. "Sorry for ever doubting you... You did bring me poison... I'm just a failure..."

He was so down in the dumps, he'd forgotten his place as a mobster.

"B-Boss... I think we might be dealing with a force to be reckoned with..."

Amidine didn't even have it in him to warn his minion about calling him that.

"So we can't off him easy, huh...? Bring it on, son... You know what to fetch me."

"Are you talking about...?"

"Yeah, the Gatling gun."

"Wha?!" The minion held his breath for a moment. "The Gatling gun... A round of its shots can make anyone into mincemeat! We can't! It's incredibly dangerous and not on the market yet—though I have no doubt it'll dominate sales in the weapons trade—and we certainly can't just show it to some civilian—!"

"Can it." Amidine's fist landed a blow on the minion's head. "Who cares? We can't have this beast roaming our streets... Let's give the newspapers something to write about. Go. Get it for me. Stat."

The minion scrambled off, head down.

A smile stretched across Amidine's lips.

"I'll rub you out this time...using our newest weapon."

Having failed to kill Lloyd once again, Amidine turned his mind to the next scene, concocting yet another scheme.

This scene was to take place in the city. Roy would be in pursuit of a large thug, who hurled passersby and stall products at him, impeding his progress. A classic foot chase.

Selen would be playing a village girl, and Phyllo, a stall vendor. They were in costume and ready.

"Hi, guys. What parts are you playing?" Lloyd asked.

"Oh, Sir Lloy—I mean, Roy! I'm supposed to be chatting at a café. Well, I won't actually be saying anything. Just pretending I'm having a conversation."

Meanwhile, Phyllo was wearing a greengrocer's outfit, grimly clutching an apple.

"...My stall gets knocked over, and I'm buried in produce."

Riho slapped them both on the backs, grinning. "Perfect roles for each of you! Phyllo's tough enough to take the fall, and from a distance, Selen *looks* normal! Flawless casting!"

Lloyd noticed Riho was in her usual clothing.

"What are you playing, Riho? You're not in costume?"

Her grin faded. "I'm helping the gaffer with the lights. It's a real pain," she grumbled.

She held up a silver board. It had a dull sheen to it.

"…What's that for?"

"It's called a bounce board." Riho sighed. "Reflects the sunlight, reduces the shadows… All part of the cinematography."

"Buck up, Riho!" Lloyd said. "Lighting is an important part of any movie! Thanks to you, I'll really get to shine!"

This brought a flush to her cheeks. "W-well, if you say so…I'll do what I can."

It was a lovely moment…soon interrupted by a heated shout.

"Well put, Roy! Your shadow is where we reside!"

Allan and the rest of the audition failures and lousy actors arrived in good spirits.

"'Sup, Roy! Allan Toin Lidocaine, captain of the bounce board brigade!"

"Allan! Wait, captain?" Lloyd asked.

Allan was now boasting of a newly minted title, but a moment before, he'd been depressed like an idol fan whose favorite was forced to retire after a shotgun wedding. How had he recovered so completely?

"Man, you sure have done a one-eighty, Allan."

"Ha! Of course I have. Amidine spoke to me in person! Said he was counting on us! We wouldn't be the Azami army if we couldn't live up to *that*!"

Amidine was almost certainly just being polite, but that had gone right to Allan's head. Only a true fanboy could get that excited just because a celebrity spoke to him.

"The depth of his courtesy! He saw we had gaffer potential! I'll become the greatest bounce board holder in Rokujou history!"

The only thing in the depths of Amidine's mind was making mincemeat of "Mr. Akizuki," but Lloyd nodded like this all made sense. Allan clapped him on the shoulder.

"Give it all you got! I once dreamed of being a famous actor—now I entrust that dream to you."

A stupid dream and a stupid request. There was nothing worse than an excitable fanboy.

"Th-thanks…but you gave me such good advice. Are you sure you don't have any regrets?"

Lloyd was taking this dumb conversation very seriously even though the right response would be to pick his nose and ignore it.

"…Don't even humor him… His nerves are frayed," Phyllo advised.

She pulled Lloyd away from Allan. It was really nice of her not to remind everyone how bad Allan's acting had been.

Then Lloyd noticed someone missing. "Uh…where's Micona?"

"Micona's playing a waitress. The guy running bumps into her and she drops a tray full of drinks. Over there, see?"

Riho pointed across the square, where Micona was standing in a cute waitress uniform…and scowling in their direction.

"Uh…she's glaring at me."

Lloyd was blissfully oblivious to the fact that Micona thought he was a home-visiting escort toying with Marie's affections, but even he had noticed she had it in for him.

"I don't think she'll do anything crazy with the cameras running, so…just focus on your performance, Ll—Roy."

Lloyd took another look at Micona, shuddered, and moved to his position.

"All right, extras from Azami, thanks for waiting! It's time for the next scene, and King Sardin's entrance!"

Sardin struck a pose. No one was sure how to react.

"Yo! King Sardin! You're the same as ever!"

"King Sardin, stop by our shop sometime!"

"Our kids are all grown up now, King Sardin!"

"King Sardin!"

He seemed quite popular with the citizens of Rokujou. They all called out to him like they would a friendly neighbor.

"Someone's popular."

"I hear everyone calls him the Dumb Dandy," Selen said. "A king who doesn't get mad, even when you don't give him the royal treatment, *would* be fairly popular."

Phyllo leaned in. "......Where's the heroine?"

Riho took out the script and looked it over.

"Uh, this scene takes place after the princess is safe, and they're trying to catch the bad guy. So the heroine isn't here. Why? Did you want her autograph?"

"...Mm."

It was unclear if that was a yes or a no.

"You're being extra weird." Riho put the script away and sat down, yawning.

Allan started yelling at her, all fired up for some reason:

"What are you doing, mercenary?! You're in the bounce board brigade! Get to your position!"

"I'm not part of your dumb brigade, nitwit! Ow! Don't shine that thing in my eyes!"

"Get to your place!" Allan yelled, desperate to share his newfound love of cinematography. "V-Formation! Stand by!"

""""Yes! Lights!""""

"V-Formation? What are we, geese? Argh, stop making this an ordeal!"

Frankly, having an array of bounce boards aimed at you in broad daylight might well set you on fire.

With his forces arranged for maximum destruction, Allan proudly reported to Sardin. "Director! Bounce boards in position!"

"Uh, sure, thanks? Just keep it down."

Allan's enthusiasm was so bad, even Sardin forgot to be the Dumb Dandy.

At this juncture, Amidine sidled up with a wicked grin.

"Sardin, a word?"

"Oh, what now, Amidine?" Sardin snapped back into character.

"You want a dozen autographs from the man soon to be the world's greatest director?"

"No, it's about the other thing," Amidine said grimly. "It's a problem for us if Mr. Akizuki can't investigate the Rising Blue Dragon."

"Certainly... How did it come to this?" Sardin shook his head.

"So," Amidine continued with a grin like an unscrupulous merchant. "What about having him injured by the villain's secret weapon, which would get him temporarily out of commission?"

"Hmm, benching him, huh...? The recasting alone has prompted a number of revisions. If we have Roy enact a last-minute miraculous recovery—and have him investigate while his character is sidelined—the sponsors' demands would be met, and so would ours!"

Sardin looked thoroughly pleased with this idea.

"We got Sardin's stamp of approval!" Amidine yelped. He was *really* falling apart here. "Okay, crew! On standby!"

He swung around, barking orders at the crew—specifically, the Rising Blue Dragon underling, who wheeled out a cloth-covered object...a Gatling gun.

"My word, that is ominous!" Sardin cried. "It looks so real... Is it safe?"

"Come now, there's little difference between a prop and the real thing!"

Amidine wasn't even making excuses at this point, and Sardin looked genuinely rattled, but Amidine only had eyes for Lloyd. His sinister grin ratcheted up another notch.

"Roy, in this next scene, you'll be taken down by the enemy's secret weapon and sidelined—temporarily."

This news took Lloyd by surprise.

"You're sure? What kind of weapon?"

"Yeah, it'll all make sense in the end. As for the weapon... Well, that's a surprise!"

Amidine flashed a nasty grin and left. Riho and Selen tried to comfort Lloyd.

"The sudden change of leads caused a lot of problems. Nobody wants to piss off the sponsors."

"Hang in there, Sir Lloy—Roy!"

Despite his grown-up body, Lloyd did his usual adorable fist pump.

"I see! Well, sudden changes or not, I've just gotta do my best!"

Both girls' heartstrings fluttered. As they clutched their chests, reeling, Phyllo swept in like the wind, catching them.

"…Mm."

"Th-thanks, Phyllo. But why did they both suddenly swoon?" Lloyd asked.

Because a man who is both handsome and doesn't know it is a killer combo.

Holding the girls upright, Phyllo shot Lloyd her customary blank stare and asked, "…The heroine… What's she like?"

"Huh? Mina? She's very classy and refined. Why do you ask?"

"…Well—"

Before Phyllo could answer, a crew member yelled out, "Places, everyone!"

"Oh, sorry, Phyllo." Lloyd dashed off to his mark.

"……It can't be her," Phyllo whispered and went to her own.

"That home-hopping escort! Marie was bad enough, but he's toying with girl after girl! He must be punished!"

In her frilly waitress uniform, Micona was seething with rage, all directed at Lloyd—or at Roy Akizuki anyway.

"All right! Sardin's own personal action movie—for Rokujou! Start!"

"Okay, scene thirty-three! Five, four, three…"

The chase scene began.

"Arghhhhhh!"

Bellowing, the large actor playing the villain ran off with Lloyd in pursuit. He knocked over a greengrocer's stand with Phyllo inside, trying to slow Lloyd down.

Lloyd dodged it easily. Just as the villain seemed cornered, he reached the secret weapon just added to the script.

"I knew this would happen! That's why my minions prepared *this*!"

"…A secret weapon here doesn't actually make sense, Amidine. Oh well…," Sardin muttered.

The middle of a city street sure was a strange place to stash a weapon, but the extras playing minions yanked the cloth off the Gatling gun. Unaware of recent advances in weapons technology, the people around just thought it was some sort of cannon with lots of narrow tubes.

As the weapon turned its sights on Lloyd, Amidine grinned, heedless of any eyes on him.

"…Prepare to meet your end, mister!"

The actor playing the villain did as he'd been told and pulled the trigger. A spray of bullets fired, spent shells flying.

"Yiiiikes! What is this thing?"

The roar of the gun and the vibrations surprised the actor so much, he slipped out of character.

The crowd around forgot they were filming, clapping their hands over their ears.

"What the— That thing's firing real ammo!" Riho growled—but the roar of the gun drowned her out.

When that hail of bullets struck Lloyd…

"Ooh, gotcha, gotcha… Gosh, these are really hot."

He wasn't sure what to make of it, so he just caught all of them.

All several hundred.

He was left with fistfuls of bullets, unsure what to do.

"Uh… Now what? A machine that lightly tosses bits of iron can't possibly be the secret weapon, can it?"

To Lloyd's mind, nobody could possibly die of a few gentle taps from these lumps of metal—of course, they would, normally, and the taps were anything but gentle.

""""Huh…?"""""

As Sardin, Amidine, and everyone else watching gaped at Lloyd's performance, a figure burst out of the shadows, hurtling toward him.

"DIEEEEEEEEEE!"

A waitress in a frilly uniform, a tray balanced on one hand—Micona, face twisted into a demonic scowl.

Lloyd tossed the bullets away, blocking her blow.

"Micona?"

"Nice block, home-invading escort! You may be scum, but you're not an Azami soldier for nothing!"

She spun the tray on one finger, then threw it at him with the full power of her buff spell, *Godspeed*. Lloyd dodged the blow easily—and realization dawned, incorrectly obviously.

"Oh! So *you're* the secret weapon, Micona! That makes more sense!"

"How dare you speak my name, privacy-invading escort?!" Micona whipped out restaurant silverware—a knife *and* a fork—and unleashed a flurry of blows like she was dual-wielding swords.

Stab, deflect, stab, stab. She was moving too fast for the eye to see, aiming for the veins on Lloyd's throat and thighs, totally going for the kill. Naturally, Lloyd wasn't even scratched.

The action was so incredible, the crowd could only stand and watch.

Even Amidine was left gaping at it, snot running down his face.

"How...did the Gatling gun do nothing? And now another Azami soldier's trying to kill him? If I wanna kill him, I've gotta find somebody *this* strong? Is he trying to get on my nerves?"

To Amidine, this was a battle between two warriors on the same side—a demonstration of skill designed to intimidate opponents into submission.

"Dammit... Fine, I'll send in my trump card—Ubi the assassin!"

Amidine failed to wipe his nose but decided to take the challenge offered.

Meanwhile, Lloyd thought this was all part of the script and decided it was probably time he lost the fight.

"Uh-oh!" he exclaimed, staggering somewhat unconvincingly. With a truly unhinged smile, Micona thrust her fork into him.

"You've visited your last home, escort!"

"Not on my watch!"

In his moment of peril, he was inexplicably saved by a random village girl—Selen. Using her cursed belt, she made a flamboyant entrance—and the ensuing action was so spectacular, a gasp of admiration went up from the crowd.

"Selen Hemein? Why?"

"A foolish question, Micona!" Selen grinned.

"Isn't anyone gonna stop this?" Riho asked.

She received no reply. People were too busy watching the action, gawking at the unscripted ad-libs, or assuming that Sardin had ordered all of this. Sardin's mind had completely shut down. Even Amidine was just standing there, watching, snot dangling from his nose. No one was in control.

"Quit slacking, Riho! The bounce board brigade is unfazed by anything!"

"We should be fazed by *this*!"

Allan was all fired up by his gaffer duties, keeping his bounce board raised high… He was dumb like that.

Micona and Selen fought on, oblivious to their surroundings. Ignoring Lloyd's consternation, they grinned at each other.

"I do admire your dedication, Selen Hemein."

"I feel closer to you knowing you're a bathroom peeper, Micona."

A tender moment between two stalkers, but they needed to remember that the cameras were still rolling.

"Then why," Micona roared, a vein throbbing on her forehead, "do you protect this malevolent escort?! What happened to your love for Lloyd Belladonna?"

"Isn't it obvious? This man…*is* Sir Lloyd!" Selen grabbed Lloyd by the face, hauling him in front of Micona.

Micona frowned, peering into his eyes. She reached out and tugged his eyebrow.

"Are you *really* Lloyd Belladonna?"

"Uh, yes," he squeaked out, unsure what else to do. "I'm just…bigger now."

©Nao Watanuki

There was a long silence.

Then the murderous aura around Micona somehow got even worse.

"Prepare to die!!"

With that unsettling shriek, Micona set her frilly skirt fluttering as she launched herself at him, exposing a bit too much to the camera lens, which was still rolling, mind you!

So the escort toying with Marie's heart was the man Micona hated most!

She was now twice as angry! Two flames of fury were merging into one very infuriated inferno!

"Vritra! Micona's inexplicably angry! Stop her!"

"Inexplicably? You didn't step on a land mine, Mistress; you dug it up and hit her with it!"

"Vritra," Selen growled.

"Roger! At once!"

Vritra was the guardian beast of Kunlun, currently possessing Selen's belt. He quickly moved to restrain Micona.

Micona, however, was in a nigh-trancelike state, hurling everything she had at Lloyd.

"Now I just have to kill one, not two! I can't believe you would make yourself bigger, just because you know you can't satisfy Marie with your little body!"

Heedless of the public eye, Micona shouted unsubstantiated innuendo, tears streaming from her eyes...

Slither...crack, crack, crack... Tree roots shot out, an insectoid shell wrapping around her.

"Crap!" Riho yelled. "Micona! You're starting to unleash the demon lords' power with everyone watching!"

"Huh? Demon lords? Why demon lords?!" Sardin asked.

The crowd was totally lost at this point. "Is this some sort of special effect?" someone asked.

Micona was way past caring. Cackling wildly, she freed herself from the belt, lunging at Lloyd...

"You will die here on foreign soil, Lloyd Belladonna! And I will comfort Marie— Aughhhh!"

Allan had aimed his bounce board right in her eyes, saving his master.

"I never would have guessed Roy was Lloyd! Bounce board brigade! Circle around! Time to rescue Lloyd!"

""""Yes! Lights!""""

The whole team started aiming light at Micona's eyes. Note to all good kids and bad ones: Don't try this one at home.

"My eyes... My eyes!"

"Now! Restrain her before she rampages further!"

Well aware of how dangerous Micona could be, the soldiers from Azami piled on top of her.

"Vritra, bind her tight! This is my chance to grab grown-up Sir Lloyd and his grown-up bits... Oooww!"

"...Mm."

Selen attempted to touch him a little in the confusion, but Phyllo threw a bounce board at her. This, obviously, was another move that neither good kids nor bad ones should attempt.

"My eyes! ...My eyes...," Selen shrieked.

"Sorry, Mistress...I was too busy binding her to save you..."

With Vritra wrapped around Micona, Selen's face had been wide open, and the corner of the bounce board dug into her skin. Selen and Micona were both left clutching their eyes.

"Nice!" Riho cried. "Guys! Restrain the shames of Azami!"

All the extras rushed in, grabbing the two idiots.

"Uh... What should I be doing?" Lloyd asked, totally left out.

"You make a run for it! Get far away from here!" Riho shouted. "Until this all dies down! Go! Get!"

"Oh, so that's what they meant by 'sidelines'! Got it! I'll run away! Like a scared rabbit!"

Lloyd spun around and vanished into the distance.

*　　*　　*

"She said to go far away…but *how* far?"

He'd gone all the way to the edge of the city.

Maybe taking Riho's instructions a bit too literally, Lloyd was now wandering Rokujou's back alleys. This area was like the East Side of Azami—not well maintained and filled with the unsavory.

"Uh, that's a dead end…I'll have to take the roofs."

Lloyd hopped lightly onto the roof above, like a ninja.

"Now, then…mm?" His ears picked up a commotion down below: running footsteps and guttural voices.

"Don't let her get away!"

"She went down there!"

"What's that? Are they filming here, too?"

Just below the roof Lloyd was standing on, a girl turned the corner with several dangerous-looking men on her heels.

Lloyd recognized her, and his eyes widened in surprise.

That's…Mina!

People were chasing his beautiful but mysterious costar! She leaned against a wall, sweating and swearing under her breath.

"Argh… Can't run in these shoes…"

"We've got her! You stole something from Amidine, right? We'll beat an answer out of ya if we hafta! Come at me, bro!"

"Hahh…hahh… Man, film crews these days are rough, huh? No way you guys are upright citizens." She looked exhausted, but her tone made it clear she wasn't defeated yet.

"An upright citizen? …Come at me, bro!" one man said, looming over her.

"Is that all you can say? Or are you shouting to disguise your insecurities? Or your guilty conscience? I have neither, so I can't relate."

"I'm not… Dammit!"

"It's cute that you took that seriously." She grinned…and started casting water magic. "Take that!"

A spear of water hurtled toward the men. But…

"No such luck, lady!"

One of the men snatched a magic stone out of his pocket and absorbed the water spear with it.

"…Tch, who'd think a film crew was carrying anti-magic weapons around with 'em?"

Seeing Mina's frown, the man grinned triumphantly.

"Film crews gotta be ready for anything these days."

"Oh, please. You're using the film profits to fund weapon development and smuggling… For the Rising Blue Dragon."

"…Was gonna let you off the hook if you gave the pendant back, but I guess that's no longer an option."

The men had her surrounded.

Lloyd was watching all this from the roof.

They're filming, right? I guess this is the subplot? Where's the camera? This wasn't in the script.

He was lost in his usual misunderstandings. He looked around, trying to find the cameras.

They'd be mad if I jumped in blindly and ruined the shot… From this angle, I imagine the camera might be over there?

The crowd of ruffians spotted him.

"Hey! Who's up there?"

"Ah! They saw me! Argh…"

He hopped down off the roof, hanging his head. This was over a dozen-yard drop, and it kinda freaked the Rising Blue Dragons out.

"Wh-what's your deal?!"

"S-sorry, I'm just a little lost."

"Nobody climbs on a roof when they're lost! You think you can lie to us? Wait, you're…"

A wave of surprise ran through the ruffians. This was the man Amidine had been trying to kill all morning—the assassin from Azami, Mr. Akizuki.

"Amidine still hasn't killed you? Even with the Gatling gun?"

"Amidine? I knew it!" Mina said.

One of the men winced.

As if he'd heard none of this, Lloyd just bowed low. "Sorry! I know you're filming!"

This just confused everyone.

"Don't play dumb! We know who you are! *Sorry* ain't cutting it!"

"Huh?"

"You ain't talking your way out of this one! Think about it!"

Lloyd thought about it. *Um, this is clearly not a real-life situation. And Mina's here...so is this an improv exercise?*

It clearly wasn't.

Oh! Mina's in the middle of an extended ad-lib! And when I showed up, they just made me a part of it! It's obvious! They got mad when I said sorry because that wasn't how they want the scene to go! I've gotta follow Allan's improv rules!

Those really don't apply here. No one should believe everything Allan said anyway.

Now convinced they were doing an improv exercise as an acting warm-up, Lloyd resolved to do his best not to disrupt the flow of the scene.

Mina, meanwhile, was trying to get him to escape.

"Roy! Run for it, they're..."

"Shut up, toots!" a man roared, brandishing a knife.

Lloyd caught his arm—moving too fast for the eye to see.

"Ah! What're you— Augh!"

The man's arm twisted. The sheer force of Lloyd's grip caused the knife to slip out of the man's hand. It clattered on the pavement below.

"Think about it, huh?" Lloyd said, his voice suddenly a low growl.

The men and Mina were equally surprised by this sudden transformation.

"Wh-who are you?!"

"I thought about it, and I decided I'd rather save the girl. Seems like the right thing to do here."

"Wh-what are you talking about?" Mina yelped. "Run for it! If they target you—"

Lloyd just flashed her an impish grin. "Don't worry," he said, playing his role to the hilt. "They'll play along and willingly lose to me."

"Like hell we will!"

Assuming he was winding them up, they pulled out weapons and charged.

Thnk! The man's blackjack struck Lloyd right in the cheek.

Weapon digging into his face, Lloyd muttered, "I'm impressed again! Professional actors really know how to pull their punches!"

"What are you— Augh!"

"Right." Lloyd lightly twisted the blackjack like he was turning a doorknob.

The man holding it spun through the air, landing headfirst on the pavement…and didn't move again.

"Huh?"

"Wow, I barely moved at all, but he did that huge pratfall! Headfirst, too! Professionals are on another level."

Lloyd's idea of "barely moved" was strong enough to heft a boulder. It would send anyone flying.

"D-drop dead!"

This time they pulled a gun. Several shots rang out in the alley.

Holes opened in Lloyd's forehead, chest, and stomach. Mina shrieked.

"Eek! Y-you've been—"

But Lloyd stayed upright. Naturally! These peashooters did no more damage to Lloyd than the corner of a desk would do the average butt.

"I've been thinking these are really impressive props! They look so real but don't hurt at all! Oops, sorry, I'm slipping out of character."

"Y-you're a monster!"

"I'll leave that to your imagination—not that you'll have time for it!"

With that cool one-liner, Lloyd went for a leg sweep, which was so fast it caused a shock wave.

One, two, three men were sent flying into the alley wall.

"Only you left, huh? Well? Ready to run?"

Instead, the man pulled out a large tube, pointing it at Lloyd.

"You're too much! But our brand-new magic stone cannon will finish you! You'll be crying for mercy!"

"Oh? Fascinating. Go on and try it." Lloyd held up a hand, waving him on.

"Y-y-y…you asked for it! I'll blow you and the dame away!"

A thunderous boom echoed through the alley. Once again, Lloyd was completely uninjured. He'd soaked up the blast with his palm… and was now lightly brushing the soot off.

"—!" The man let out a voiceless shriek.

"Er, really? No damage at all? How?" Mina asked.

"How? I dunno, I just work out," Lloyd explained. *That seems like something they'd say in movies*, he thought.

Then he took a swing at the last of the ruffians. He was sent helplessly ragdolling away and slumped unconscious against the far wall.

"Wow," Lloyd breathed out. "A light little tap and his eyes rolled back in his head! He's a real pro."

"R-Roy?" Mina asked. "Who are you? They said something about knowing who you are?"

He was not prepared for that at all.

"Er, um…," he stammered, at a loss.

"You can't tell me, huh? Fair enough. But you'd better wash your hands of this mess, fast. You won't last long in Rokujou with the Rising Blue Dragon on your heels."

"Oh! We're still using that story line."

"Story line?"

"Er, I mean…huh?"

There was a commotion from down the alley. Were they cops running toward the fight? Or backup for the ruffians?

"Crap, it's the cops—they've got the police in their pocket. They won't help us."

"Oh, one of *those* stories. Then if you'll excuse me…"

"Huh? Eaugh! Wait, not so fast! I'm not ready!"

Sweeping Mina into his arms, Lloyd beat a hasty retreat, leaping from rooftop to rooftop.

As the sun set, they arrived at a park by the coast, and Lloyd gently set her down. It was getting quite dark.

Mina's eyes were frozen all the way open, staring at him.

"You're not the first person I've met with skills like that. Phyllo, and… You're sure you don't have a brother?"

"Something the matter?"

"…No, just talking to myself."

"Okay…well, I'd better get back. I dunno where I was supposed to wait…"

Lloyd vanished like the wind.

"Roy Akizuki… Roy… He was so…warm."

Mina spoke his name like she was shielding the embers in her heart from the sea breeze. Then she remembered the pendant she'd hidden at her chest and held it up to the moonlight.

"I can't get distracted. Not until I've used this pendant to save my mother. I don't have much time. Every moment counts."

Lloyd was headed back the way he'd come, returning to the shoot.

"Was that enough time? Maybe too much? I'd better get back."

Lloyd reached the shopping district and looked around, wondering which way to go next. Then he felt eyes on him from a side street.

"—?"

He turned to look.

"………"

Across the main path was a woman standing by the side of the road, staring directly at him.

Blond hair. Skin so pale it was almost sickly. She wore an ordinary jacket and jeans—easy to move in. Lloyd recognized her.

"The woman from the photo!"

The one Sardin had showed him. This was Ubi—Sardin had called her his wife.

A carriage passed between them.

The moment his view of her was obscured, she vanished.

"…Did she go down the alley? Does she want me to follow?"

She'd left only a faint trail for him to track—traces of dust, sounds of movement up ahead. He moved farther down the narrow alley. As the noises of the main drag faded, the path opened up, and he found her sitting on a pile of scrap wood. This seemed to be a vacant lot, abandoned mid-construction. There was more than enough room—and it was quiet enough—for a fight.

"You didn't hesitate to follow," she called out.

"Um," Lloyd said, tensing up. "You seemed to want me to follow you, so… Was I wrong?"

Ubi's eyes widened slightly at his response, but that look soon faded. "…Bluff all you like."

This pale woman had taken his nerves as an act, one designed to make her underestimate him.

"That won't work on me," she warned.

Lloyd hadn't been trying anything of the sort, so he was just confused.

Then he found a knife at his throat.

The wind whistled.

Without any sign or sound of her advance, Ubi's blade was upon him. Anyone else would have died without even realizing what had happened.

Lloyd sidestepped it easily.

"……!" She shifted her grip, swinging again—and once more, Lloyd made it look effortless.

"Tch!"

He'd deflected Ubi's blow with such speed, she lost her balance and went down on one knee.

She was back on her feet and attacking again in no time. Now using walls and wood piles as footholds, she came at him from all directions, trying to slip past Lloyd's guard.

"At these speeds, even you can't—!"

Her knife hurtled toward Lloyd's temple.

"Whoa!"

Lloyd caught the blade between two fingers like it was easy. It was clearly not humanly possible. Ubi leaped backward, suddenly cautious.

"…You're good," she noted, astonished.

Lloyd was every bit as surprised. *She just attacked me…and took a pretty big fall when I deflected it lightly… Ohhh!*

Lloyd straightened up, calling out to her.

"You're Ubi, right?"

She answered with silence.

"Thank you for helping me out!" he said, bowing low.

"Huh?" She frowned, genuinely rattled now.

Lloyd didn't notice at all. He just looked up, an expression of deep gratitude on his face.

"You're trying to improve my acting, right? You're the producer!"

"The…producer? What's that?"

"Sardin called you his wife during our improv scene the other day. That was a metaphor! I've heard the director is the father and the producer is the mother!"

"Sardin said… What is he *doing*?" Ubi clutched her forehead, unable to keep up with Lloyd's multiple layers of distortion. "…Are you serious, or is this some sort of joke? I've never met anyone this hard to deal with."

Like a sales rep trying to serve an incoherent customer, she was clearly giving up on her usual playbook.

"You saw how bad I was at action scenes and invited me here to help!" Lloyd exclaimed, proud of himself for figuring it out. "Thank you so much! You're a great actor yourself! I really thought you were an assassin trying to kill me!"

Lloyd was all ready for a one-on-one lesson on how to pull off stunts.

The only thing he was right about was the part where she *had* been trying to kill him.

"You...mean every word of that?" Ubi asked, clutching her head.

"Yes! I think you're marvelous! You might be producing this film, but you're actually an action film actress, right? The way you use these props—I can't wait to get started! What page of the script are we on?"

"Actress? Props? Script?" Ubi squeaked, panic rising with each word.

Then she forced herself to calm down, lowered her center of gravity, and brandished her knife.

"You may weave a cloud of confusion with your words, but I'm not letting that distract me."

The moonlight glinted off her blade.

"I must slay you here for the sake of my family."

"Uh...was that line in the script?"

The more serious Ubi got, the more Lloyd's reactions ruined it all, and she was getting increasingly frustrated by this.

Lloyd had pulled the script out of his pocket, oblivious to her frustration. He flipped through it, searching for that line. Then...

"It's not in here! Then it must be improv! Oh, this is great for my action-movie training!"

Improv was like a magic word for Lloyd now.

"Blabbing about training and acting won't rattle—!" Ubi started, but Lloyd had launched into his own version of "movie action."

"Hah!" He'd scooped up a rusty nail from the ground and hurled it at her.

A nail had been lying there, buffeted by wind and rain for days on end…and he threw it with such force, it buried itself in a brick wall like a shotgun shell.

"Huh?"

Before Ubi could recover from her shock, Lloyd was already improvising more action with nearby objects.

"How about this mop?" he asked, snatching up an old abandoned mop—the kind you use to clean grime and moss off walls. He twirled it like a baton, somewhat inexpertly.

Ubi raised her knife, assuming he was gonna hit her with it. "I can handle a mop," she said. It was better than a rusty nail bullet anyway.

"If I charge the mop with power…hah!"

"Huh? Power?"

At Lloyd's yelp, the mop ends began writhing and then sharpened into pointy spikes.

"Coming in hot!" Lloyd took that bed of spikes and swung it right at her, no hesitation at all.

Ubi desperately fled the whirlwind his swing kicked up, ducking low against the wall. She'd come in like a beautiful badass, but there was no trace of that left at all.

"Th-that was close!"

Terrified, she looked up at the wall above her…and saw a gouge in it, like someone had taken a spoon to ice cream.

"That's a mop, right? Just a mop?!"

"I just copied a lady from my neighborhood, but it went real well!" Lloyd exclaimed happily.

"What kind of neighbors do you have?!"

Kunlun ladies regularly used brooms to dispatch dust *and* demon lords.

Their battle raged on—perhaps leaning toward the comedy side of action-comedy.

The sounds of it reached another woman, who came racing to the scene.

"Hahh…hahh…hahh…"

The mysterious actress, Mina! Clutching her pendant tight, still in costume, she was trying to catch her breath.

"Huh? Mina?"

"I heard a racket, got a bad feeling, and came running…and it *is* you. And…"

Her eyes locked on Lloyd's opponent—Ubi.

Ubi said nothing.

"Er, um, this is…Ubi," Lloyd introduced. "She's teaching me about movie stunts!"

Mina point-blank ignored Lloyd's delusions.

"What are you *doing*, Mom?" she asked, on the verge of tears.

"Huh? Mom? Is this industry jargon for the producer?"

Ubi did not appear the least bit fazed by Mina's entrance.

"……Natie."

"I've been looking everywhere! I heard you were dead, but I didn't believe it! I became a mercenary and scoured Rokujou for you… If you're alive, get word to me!"

"…" Ubi maintained her silence.

"Say something!" Mina roared. "I thought your last client was suspicious! So I disguised myself as an actress to get closer to Amidine…and finally had a lead, but you just ran off! Why? Why are you working for the mob?!"

Mina looked ready to burst into tears. Ubi was looking increasingly sad, too.

Lloyd was watching, totally left out.

Wow! So this is how professionals do it—by taking the "producer is a movie's mother" thing to its logical extreme!

He was getting everything wrong again. The Mom thing *had* been genuinely unexpected.

Ubi fought to keep the sadness off her face, raising the knife.

©Nao Watanuki

"Sorry, but I'm no longer a mother. Go back home. Or else—"

"—! You can't mean that!"

Tension crackled.

Lloyd had just been standing there this whole time, but…

—! *Oh! I shouldn't just watch! I've got to contribute! I need to be better at ad-libbing!*

Being selected for a lead role was an important duty. He adjusted his performance to fit the serious vibe.

"You shouldn't lie, Ubi," he growled.

"What?!" Ubi yelped, caught off guard by his sudden transformation. She turned the knife toward him.

"You think she's lying, Roy?"

"I've seen a lot of people in this line of work," Lloyd said. "But you're the worst liar I've ever met."

"…You're just making stuff up now. You won't get away with it."

"Did you think I wouldn't notice that look in your eyes? The look of a mother proud to see how her daughter's grown? That's why you've involved yourself here! You've seen every movie Mina's been in, bought the pamphlet—two copies, one to read and one to keep."

Lloyd was not hesitating to put any idea that crossed his mind into this ad-lib…

"H-how did you know that?!"

By some miracle, he was exactly right. Ubi had turned bright red. She'd *clearly* bought two pamphlets.

What a pro! Playing along with my idea like that… It's amazing.

Lloyd was getting carried away. He decided to double down on his improvisation.

"You even come to watch her filming every chance you get… You're there five days out of every week she films."

"G-gah…" Ubi hid her face, at a loss for words.

"Really, Mom? Five—?" Mina asked.

"Not five!" Ubi protested, clearly mortified. "More like four—three!"

So Lloyd was right on the money.

"Whatever you say out loud, inside, you're still her mom."

Lloyd might just be ad-libbing, but it sure had changed the tone of this encounter. It was now quite pleasant—enough that Ubi was forced to grudgingly admit the truth.

"W-well, uh…you know, I was worried!"

"Really? Mom!" Mina looked delighted. She stepped closer.

"Why would I not be worried? You became an actress to find me. You started sniffing around the Rising Blue Dragon…and then you started getting famous."

Ubi suddenly spun to face Lloyd, looking for anything to take the spotlight off herself.

"And you!" she snapped.

"Er, yes?" Lloyd squeaked, forgetting to act.

"You and Natie seem awfully comfortable. Are you two close?"

This came out of nowhere, but since Lloyd thought this was all an improv exercise…

Uh, um…right! I can't say no here!

Allan's rules were ironclad. He replied immediately.

"She's certainly important to me."

A puff of steam shot out of Mina's ears.

"Whaaaa? Y-you mean…whaaaaa?"

The sudden romantic confession had totally blindsided her.

"Looks like I'm right," Ubi said, a smirk appearing on her lips. "Sorry I attacked you. Look after her for me. I can't guarantee your safety, though… Ask Sardin to get you two as far from here as possible."

"No! You have to come with us! And why would King Sardin—?"

Then Mina saw someone coming up the path.

"I figured I'd keep an eye on things—but this explains everything. The rising star was your daughter? No wonder she was poking her nose in my affairs."

It was Amidine. He was clapping as he spoke.

"So you *are* the boss of the Rising Blue Dragon!" Mina snarled, bracing herself.

Amidine grinned. "That I am! What about it?"

"Amidine...she's..."

"I won't harm her. We need the movie business to be a success! Can't go losing young talent."

Amidine turned to glare at Lloyd.

"But there you have it, Mr. Akizuki. If you want your beloved Mina and her mother to live, I'll have you bow out here. They matter more than your mission, right?"

"What are you talking about? There's...there's nothing between— and it's three against one! You're the one who should be bowing out!"

Mina started casting a water spell.

Amidine faced her down.

And Ubi stepped between them, face twisted in anguish.

"Mom? Why?!"

Amidine cackled. "This woman? She's already dead."

Amidine pulled a bloodred jewel out of his pocket, grinning.

"The power to control the living dead...I killed this woman and used necromancy to bring her back to life! She's my own personal zombie!"

"Gah!"

Amidine must have used the jewel to command her. Ubi pulled out her knife and placed it to her own throat, grimacing.

"Mom! Stop!"

"Sorry, Natie..."

"But if her head and torso are severed, she'll be gone for good. Well? Willing to give up on ever speaking to your mom again?"

Mina grit her teeth but let the water spell dissipate.

"Heh, you had to do this the hard way. Right, Mr. Akizuki, after that little demonstration, do you still plan to fight?"

"Roy...I'm sorry..."

"So says the girl you love. Are you ready...to die for her?"

Amidine pulled out a gun. This was nothing like the one he'd used before—it was much bulkier and clearly far more powerful.

"Huh? Is that some sort of portable camera? Is the film stored inside it somehow?"

"You fool!" He pulled the trigger, and there was a thunderous crack. Lloyd's face exploded.

"R-Roy!"

Lloyd was flung backward into the wall behind him. Smoke rose from his face. It smelled of burning flesh...and was a sight grisly enough to make anyone want to look away. His body slid down the side of the building, crumpling in a heap on the ground.

Amidine glanced down at the barrel of his weapon.

"A portable bazooka—what a ridiculous machine. Who *are* our sponsors? This made barbecue of his face. If bullets to the chest and face don't work, then I gotta blow his face clean off... This time, it *must* have been fatal. Oww..."

He rubbed his hand. The kick must have been pretty nasty.

Mina gave him a look of fury, but he just grinned at her.

"You're gonna be a movie star!" he exclaimed. "Don't look so scary."

"I would never—!"

"Sorry, but the movie business demands it. Whatever your motives, people are responding. And your mother wants you kept happy...so don't fight it. If I die, the necromancy ends, and you can say good-bye to your mom's soul as it goes on up to heaven."

Amidine waved the jewel in Ubi's direction.

Unable to control herself, Ubi hit Mina in the side of her neck. She crumpled to the ground.

"Wow, your mom really doesn't hold back!"

"—! You forced me to—"

Amidine reached down, scooping up an item that had come spilling out of Mina's shirtfront.

"Whew, she was really a step away—close one."

"What is that pendant? Stealing things now? Like a petty thief?"

"Aww, don't be like that! This was mine to begin with. But I'm in a good mood, so I'll let it pass. Nothing feels better than finishing off an enemy with your own two hands. Haven't felt this good since I killed the last boss! Be proud of that, Mr. Akizuki."

With a sinister chuckle, Amidine walked away. Ubi gave her unconscious daughter a look of sorrow—and followed after.

A few minutes later…

"Uh…was that the right improv choice?"

Lloyd just got up like nothing was wrong. He took a handkerchief out and wiped the soot off his face. It had the *disenchant* rune stitched into it, so he was soon back to normal.

"Man, real actors and producers sure are intense—I really felt like he was a mafia boss! Oh, Mina!"

Lloyd held Mina up, patting her cheeks.

But she didn't wake up.

"Uh…did she fall asleep? We did start shooting awfully early. Being a movie actress must take its toll on your body…"

He decided to pick her up and carry her back to the cadets' lodgings.

"I can't just leave her here. We can put her up in one of our rooms… but I'm still in my grown-up form! Wait, everyone knows about that now. I can go like this… Still, she looks awfully familiar…"

Especially with her eyes closed, she looked like someone he knew. Trying to place it, Lloyd leaped from building to building.

Bounding across the moonlit sky, it only took grown-up Lloyd a few minutes to reach their hotel.

His friends were waiting outside, worried by his late return.

"Lloyd…Belladonna…I will crush you!"

"Now, now, Micona. Selen, keep that belt tight."

"Geez…you're the worst kind of stalker," Selen grumbled.

"Like you're any better, Belt Princess! Where is Lloyd? I need to apologize!"

"……Anyone have any sedatives?"

At least one of this crew was less worried than gunning for his life.

Lloyd landed softly in front of them. The sight of his handsome face floating down out of the night sky made Selen's heart skip a beat.

"Oh, Sir Lloyd! You've come by moonlight to whisk me away from here!"

But her fantasy faded the moment she noticed his arms had an occupant—Mina, unconscious. Selen's heart skipped several more beats—almost stopping entirely.

"M'lady, don't have a heart attack yet!" Riho said, giving her chest compressions. Selen pulled through…and immediately demanded answers.

"Sir Lloyd! Why are you clutching a movie star in your arms?! Why is she asleep?! I am the only heroine in your life—!"

Phyllo took a vise grip on a chunk of Selen's cheek flesh, stopping her.

"…Mina?" She squinted at the sleeping actress.

"L-Lloyd! You're so grown up! In several ways!" Allan shrieked. "I never thought you'd become a *real* man! I must apologize for my behavior the other day! And I swear to live by your example! Ow! Help!"

The conclusions Allan had leaped to had earned him the ire of every girl present. Lots of feet stomping on his toes. Ow.

"But seriously, Lloyd, what's going on?" Riho asked. "You didn't really—"

Before she could even finish, Choline floated out of the gate, eyes totally dead.

"Lights out, kids."

"Oh, sorry, Colonel Choline! This is kind of important."

"Lights out."

"Uh…Colonel? What's going on with you? Yesterday you were all angry; today you've like, achieved nirvana?"

"Oh, nothing. Just here I am in Rokujou, but I can't even have a drink, go outside, sleep, do anything! I oughtta sue somebody."

"Clearly you have hardships of your own…"

"It's not fair! And you're all having fun where I can see it? That's a crime! Get back to your rooms."

Rokujou had asked them to come help, but two full days had passed without anyone getting in touch with her. She'd spent that whole time on edge and was well past her limit. She was seriously one step away from turning evil.

She turned and drifted off down the hall, growling, "Any naughty children still awake?" like a child-eating monster.

"Sorry, Mina isn't waking up... I couldn't just leave her there, so I brought her back with me."

Riho looked relieved to hear this. "That's what I figured!"

"You were the most upset, Riho Flavin," Micona observed, peering out from her bondage.

"*Hngg*," Riho moaned, unable to refute that accusation.

"I don't give a goddamn who Lloyd Belladonna hooks up with—as long as it isn't Marie—but you should probably find a bed for that girl."

For once, Micona was actually being mature and offering good advice.

"Yeah, we can figure out what's going on once she wakes up. Don't wanna piss Colonel Choline off, either...and Allan looks half-dead..."

"...Mm." Phyllo took Mina from Lloyd and started off indoors, almost at a run.

"Yo, Phyllo! What's the hurry?"

"......Mm."

With her usual indecipherable grunt, Phyllo vanished into her room.

"'Mm' doesn't tell us crap! Only Mena can figure those out..."

"Come, Riho, back to our rooms. Oh, Sir Lloyd, our room is this way—"

"Don't try and sneak him in with you!"

"We'd better get back. Colonel Choline'll chew us out... If someone could lend me a shoulder..." Allan groaned.

"And untie me?" Micona asked.

As they all headed back to their rooms, Lloyd was still stuck on Mina's sleeping face.

"I swear I've seen it before...the way her eyes close..."

Thinking about it wasn't getting him anywhere. He decided going to bed earlier would help him get ready for tomorrow's shoot.

Meanwhile, in Amidine's apartment...

Face flushed from the bottle of well-aged wine he'd downed, Amidine dove into bed.

"Heh-heh-heh...I can finally sleep again! I'm back in the lead role! Rising Blue Dragon will continue to rule Rokujou from the shadows! I'll get everything I ever wanted and live a life of fulfillment! Can't wait for tomorrow."

He was so wound up, he was downright out of character! The following day was shaping up to be fun.

In the morning, Amidine rolled out of bed feeling great to be alive. His eyes were a bit puffy, likely from the wine.

As he smoked his morning cigarette, he spoke to himself in the mirror.

"Good morning, asshole. You finally killed that little shit. Heh-heh-heh."

He donned his usual suit and turned to the mirror once more.

"...It worked this time, right? He's not just gonna show up again, right?"

He waved a hand at his reflection, as if waylaying its fears.

"Pfft, don't worry, Amidine Oxo. He's finished. Even a monster like him can't survive that!"

Remembering how Lloyd had been powerless to stop his face turning to barbecue, he grinned.

"Never figured he'd fall for Mina. Made it so easy to finish him off. Even a freak like Mr. Akizuki turned out to be human in the end. Don't worry—you won't see him again. Today won't be a repeat of yesterday!"

Having Lloyd just turn up for work like nothing had happened had really been traumatizing.

Then his henchman knocked at the door, announcing the arrival of his carriage.

"Good morning, Amidine."

He'd arrived at the exact same time as the day before, which gave Amidine déjà vu…

"You couldn't have shown up earlier…or later? One or the other?"

The underling wasn't sure how to respond to that. But can you blame Amidine? He didn't want to jinx himself. Once one noticed an omen, it was hard to dismiss it.

"Uh…which is better?" his minion managed.

"Just…don't do things like we did yesterday. Please."

"Right, I'll…try. You came back late last night…"

"What did I just say?! I killed him! I got the pendant back! Don't make me say it again!"

This was hardly fair, but the minion *had* said the same thing the day before.

"Er…that's the first time I've heard any of that?" he squeaked. It was hard to know how to respond to an angry boss when you weren't sure *why* he was so wound up.

"Argh, sorry. Just…feels like you're jinxing things. Bad case of déjà vu, I guess."

"Wow, sounds like you're pretty tired…I'll wait at the carriage."

"Today is not like yesterday… It's a brand-new day… Today will be great!"

Amidine hummed a little song to himself the whole way to the shooting location, as if trying to banish his fears.

And the moment he got to set…

"Good morning!"

Lloyd was there, waiting for him.

"How are you still here?! Why did I bother humming?!" Amidine shrieked, looking ready to burst a blood vessel.

"Er...I am on time, right?"

"That's not the probleeeeeem...!"

Heedless of the crowd around him, Amidine crumpled to the ground.

Whyyyy? I shot him in the face with a bazooka! I smelled his flesh burning! It was super inappropriate, but I was left craving a good grilled steak!

"Um, is something wrong?"

How is he fine? Wait! This is just like yesterday! Am I stuck in a time loop?

Sadly, no. Lloyd had merely mistaken that for an improv exercise.

The sight of Amidine writhing on the ground was making Sardin worried.

"A-are you okay, Amidine?"

"I'm fine! I'm so not fine! But let's say I'm fine!"

"So you aren't?"

Amidine's minions on the crew were worried, too. Their boss was always impeccably confident, but not today.

"Er, Amidine?"

"What do I do? How...? My future... Everything I ever wanted... I just need a weapon that can kill him!"

Then he remembered Sou and Shouma and all the insane technology they'd happily offered.

"That's right!"

"Er, Amidine?"

"Yes! I just have to steal from them! Steal the ultimate weapon!"

Amidine leaped to his feet. All trace of his movie star aura had gone—all that was left was a hideous, insatiable ghoul.

"They're the ones who stole the lead from me... It's only right I steal something back! I'll kill them...and steal their weapon! I'll have Ubi do it... Even if she dies, I can use her daughter instead... Even use Sardin...heh...heh-heh-heh..."

"S-seriously, what ails you, Amidine?"

"Gather all the weapons! It's time for war!"

"W-war?!"

"Everyone in the underground layers! It's time we went after those sponsors and swiped everything they've got!"

His eyes locked on something far away, Amidine staggered off the set.

Chapter 4

A Jarring Plot Twist: Suppose a Tearjerker Ended with a B-Movie Comedy Punch Line

An hour after Amidine left…

A restless pall had settled over the set.

"Director, Amidine still isn't back…and several crew members vanished with him."

"Hmm… They were all veteran crew members Amidine personally hired. What's going on here?"

Sardin was left clutching his head.

Amidine leaving was one thing, but taking a dozen crew members with him? This was delaying the shoot, and he was losing his mind trying to fix things.

"I've got Roy reading the script on standby, but…argh, and Mina hasn't shown up, either! Why is this happening?!"

The cadets from Azami were hanging around, waiting for instructions.

"Mm? What are we waiting for? My soul is crying out for lighting!"

Allan was hefting a bounce board like he was lifting weights.

"Quit waving that around! You keep flashing light in my eyes. I think we're waiting for Mina? Did she wake up?" Riho asked.

"…If Mina doesn't show, someone else will have to take her part," added Selen. "*Gasp!* Is God looking out for me?!"

No situation could ever make Selen change her essential Selen-ness.

"Don't even joke about that, Selen Hemein. I just want to wrap filming up and go see Marie…"

Micona was much the same.

Then a stir ran over the set.

"What, is Amidine back?"

A female crew member ran over to Sardin, out of breath. She shook her head. "Hah…hah…no, sir."

"Then what?"

"Uh… We've got someone complaining, but I'm unsure why."

Even as she spoke, they heard a loud voice bellowing like someone who's had a few too many.

What? A drunk? Everyone turned to look…

"Wassa big deal? How long you gonna keep me waitin'?! Day after day and you never get in touch?! Huh?!"

An instructor from Azami Military Academy…Colonel Choline.

She'd been dispatched to Rokujou with secret orders and had been on standby at the inn this whole time, waiting for Sardin to contact her…which he never did. Being cooped up in her own hometown had worn her down…and now she was past the point of no return. Without the benefit of any alcohol, she was rolling up for a fight.

When her eyes locked onto Sardin, she made a beeline right for him, grabbing a fistful of his shirt.

"You! Sardin Valyl-Tyrosine, the Dumb Dandy! You asked *us* to bail you out, but you're just sitting around filming your dumb movie?!"

"C-Colonel! Don't say that so loud!"

"I'll be as loud as I want! You asked us for a favor, but don't ever bother getting in touch?! Why would I not shout?! 'Please help! Rokujou's in trouble! The Rising Blue Dragon's after me!'"

"I contacted you! I spoke to Mr. Akizuki!"

"Don't you lie to me! We don't have any Akizukis!"

This situation was clearly a huge mess, but the cadets had been briefed on none of this, so they could only watch in horror.

Another stir ran through the set.

"Y-you're—," a crew member yelled. Everyone turned to look.

"Sorry, I need to talk to King Sardin."

Mina was hanging on to Phyllo's shoulder, pushing through the crowd.

"Your Majesty, I have urgent news…"

Before she could finish, Choline blocked her way, scowling.

"Do ya, pretty lady? Too bad! I'm busy talking to this Dumb Dandy! Butt out! Go on, get! I'll win this lawsuit, trust…meeee…"

Phyllo had quietly put Choline in a sleeper hold. She passed out, still frowning, and crumpled like marionette that's lost its strings.

"Uh, Phyllo? That's a bit overboard."

"……Emergency measures."

"Emergency or not, you just knocked out a superior officer, Phyllo Quinone. And she looks very silly now! You've ruined her prospects of marriage for the foreseeable future!"

Micona smoothly added insult to injury. Even without waking up, tears formed in Choline's eyes.

But Phyllo just whispered, "…This is an emergency. For Rokujou… and the two of us."

"Us? You and Mina? When did you two get so close?"

"………Well, Mina's my sister."

""""Huh…?"""""

Phyllo reached out and gave Mina's hair a tug.

"Augh, Phyllo! I'm not ready for—"

The curly wig came off…of Mena's head.

""""Ahhhhh!"""" all the cadets from Azami yelped.

"Mena Quinone…what's going on here?" Micona demanded.

Mena was at a total loss. No trace of her usual clowning.

"Argh, I'm not getting outta this one, am I? Fine, I'll fill everybody in."

Mena's eyes became smiley—back to their default position—but she rarely sounded this serious.

"Sorry, it's kind of a long story. King Sardin, you should hear it, too."

"I'm listening." Sardin looked from Mena to Phyllo and back again.

Mena took a deep breath…and dropped a huge bombshell.

"The boss of the Rising Blue Dragon…is Amidine Oxo."

"What?!"

"I've been after them, too. And…"

Mena explained why she'd been disguised as Mina, investigating the mob, and just what evils she'd uncovered.

"Figuring Amidine was suspicious, I became an actress to get close to him."

Choline woke up halfway through that line, heard Mena was an actress, and passed out again.

"But why didn't you tell us?" Selen asked, sounding hurt. "I mean, I get that it's a family problem, but…"

Mena scratched her cheek, looking guilty. "I didn't want anyone knowing I was acting! Uh, Phyllo?"

Phyllo had leaned in very close, looking as expressionless as ever, but…there was a hint of sadness there.

"……If Mom's involved…even if it's dangerous…you should have let me know."

Mena's eyes went wide; then she winced. "Sorry. But if Mom turned out to be dead, I didn't want to disappoint you…and if I failed…I thought it would hurt less if I just went missing."

"But…!" Phyllo started to protest.

Riho grabbed her arm. "Put yourself in her shoes, Phyllo."

Phyllo bit back her words. A grim look settled over her. "Is it true that Mom's under a necromancer's spell?"

"Yeah, and I wanna save her and thwart Amidine's plans. I know it's a bit late, but…will you help, Phyllo?"

"…Mm. No more acting alone. Let's save Mom together."

All friction between them gone, they put their hands together. Those who knew them smiled approvingly.

"I'll help, too. In return, all I need's an autograph from an up-and-coming actress," Riho said.

"If you tell everyone you know how urgent it is they make a movie starring myself and Sir Lloyd, I'll happily help," Selen chimed in.

"No gaffer would ever let evil stand!" Allan shouted.

One of those was *extra* weird, but Mena ignored him, tears forming in her eyes.

"Thanks, guys… Oh! I almost forgot. Before Amidine took me away, there was someone who fell to his hand. Roy—poor Roy Akizuki."

Mena choked back her tears—remembering his body lying on the bricks, his face burned off…and nothing she could do to save him.

Sadness overwhelmed her.

Behind her, grown-up Lloyd looked up from the script he'd been writing, and—oblivious to what was going on—joined the others.

"Oh, sorry, I was so focused on the script—what are we doing?"

"Howwwwwww?!"

The dead man himself appeared with all the breezy ease of a real star dropping in on a program of celebrity impersonators.

Mena let out a howl like someone who's realized their seat belt isn't fastened just as the roller-coaster crests the first hill.

In Roy's form, Lloyd's gentle smile never wavered.

"Hmm? Mina, you changed your hair? It looks good! Reminds me of someone…"

"Y-you're alive?! He shot you at point-blank range with a bazooka! You were buried beneath a huge pile of rubble!"

Riho was starting to get the gist and figured it would save time if she just let Mena in on the trick.

"Uh, I think this'll just explain everything, so—this is Lloyd."

"Huh?"

"They have some rune that makes him look grown up. Figured it would be a good look for action scenes."

Mena blinked a few times—but she was well aware that where Kunlun was concerned, anything was possible. Her brain processed it all pretty quickly.

"Oh, so you're Lloyd. That explains—"

Then the rest of the memories caught up with her. A series of tender, romantic moments with Roy flashed before her eyes.

©Nao Watanu

"Eeaaaaaaaaaaaaaaaughhhhhhhhhhhh!"

"Er...you seem even more surprised?" Riho said, baffled. Then her eyes narrowed. "Did something happen? Oh no...you don't mean... you didn't know who he was, so..."

Before she could continue, Micona broke her silence. "Not another word, Riho Flavin!"

"What's your problem, Micona? Some things are worth spelling out!"

"...She'll hear."

"Who'll hear?"

Micona pulled open a manhole cover and used the treant power harbored within her to send roots down inside, dragging out...

"Dammit! I was just following that stupid grandma and got lost..."

Marie...covered head to foot in mud. Micona's Marie meter had gone off, and she'd fished her up.

"Ahhh! Marieee! I never imagined I would meet you abroad! This is, you know, a sign from God that we should hold the ceremony here!"

"Vritra, bind her."

"...That seems to be all I do lately."

Once the belt had saved Marie's chastity yet again, Lloyd ran up to her.

"M-Marie! Why are you here?"

"Oh, Lloyd...uh, well, Alka's rage isn't subsiding, and she'd been running all over the place all morning, and then she lost me in an underground cave, and I couldn't find my way out and accidentally wandered into some weird mafia lair, and it was awful."

"A weird mafia?!" Sardin yelped.

"Oh, the magic stone mines!" Mena exclaimed. "So they've been hiding underground...no wonder they're so hard to find!"

"It seems we've not a moment to spare," Sardin said with all the royal dignity he could muster. "Amidine has concealed his true nature for years...and if he's revealed his hand now, then whatever he's up to must be stopped at all costs! And then...Ubi will be..."

His voice dropped to a whisper at her name. But Mena and Phyllo heard him loud and clear.

"……Ubi? Why do you know Mom's name?" Phyllo asked, tilting her head to the side.

"King Sardin," Mena said, stepping closer, "I wanted to ask about that. What's your relationship with our mother?"

"Er, um…"

"When she was trying to help me escape, she said to go to you. But what's your connection to her?"

Sardin took a step back, fidgeting. Several expressions crossed his face: hesitation, sorrow, yearning.

It was clearly not something that could be explained in a word.

"Uh, Director? What exactly is going on here? Why is everyone so intense?"

"Oh, perfect timing, Roy! You see—"

Sardin turned to Lloyd, spying an escape. Mena's and Phyllo's glares stayed pinned to him, but he quickly began explaining Amidine's misdeeds and how they had to stop him.

"Oh!" Lloyd cried. "I get it."

He looked very serious. The fate of the country was on the line. The tension left a bead of sweat running down his brow.

"No need to stress it, mister," Sardin assured him. "You and your friends will be fine. I'll do all I can to help!"

"Y-you will?" Lloyd asked, surprised. Then he made up his mind and thumped his chest. "Very well! I'll tackle this mission with body and soul!"

"Thank you, Mr. Akizu—"

"The script may have changed a lot, but as the lead actor, I've got to step up!"

"Er…script?"

Sardin blinked several times. Weird. This conversation wasn't adding up. He gave Lloyd a long, searching look.

"I appreciate your concerns, but I think I get the gist! Amidine was actually playing the villain! But you tricked the whole cast and crew with a fake script! Setting up a shocking twist in the last reel!"

Given Lloyd's conviction that all of this was part of the filmmaking process, one had to admire how flexible the inner workings of his mind were. He'd successfully incorporated everything that was happening around him.

"The king and the army, filming a movie in Rokujou! In the shadows, Amidine and the Rising Blue Dragon attempt to thwart the movie production! A script that keeps changing leads, and as we race to keep up, he laughs in the shadows—and we finish with a big-budget action scene! I never realized this movie would be a mockumentary action film!"

"Er, uh…it's not a movie? You don't need to act, mister."

"Exactly! It's not just a movie anymore! You've tricked us into acting out the scenes you needed and filmed them like a documentary! I don't even need to act! I just need to be myself!"

As Sardin searched for an explanation, Choline clapped him on the shoulder.

"I'm the one here on royal degree, King Sardin. That kid…is just clueless."

"C-clueless? Uh…but…"

"He must have assumed everything was part of the scene and done his best to play along. He's such a good boy!"

As Sardin gaped at her, Lloyd put a hand in the air, speaking to everyone.

"Let's get to work! I'm here for you!"

A cheer went up. Sardin's head was still reeling, but…

"It's a lot to take on board, Your Majesty," Choline said. "But if you've got him on your team, you've won. He'll solve everything. Don't worry."

"Then… Okay. If we can save Rokujou…and her…"

He made a face like he was working through some indigestion.

Mena and Phyllo were making the same face, still waiting for an answer.

"Seriously, what's his angle?"

"...Mm."

They had no way of knowing he was their father. Mena might have had an inkling, but her rational mind was busy telling her "No way."

Meanwhile, in the sewers beneath Rokujou...

Remnants of peak magic stone mining operations visible all around, these tunnels were now used to transport both clean water into and waste water out of the city.

It was impossible to escape the stench of mold or the shrill squeaks of the rats... No one would want to be down here without good reason.

Yet, here stood a group sporting firearms, facing two very strange men.

The latter pair were Sou and Shouma, and the armed group were Rising Blue Dragon henchmen under Amidine's command.

The mob was crackling with tension, but Sou and Shouma remained perfectly relaxed.

"You said you were here to give us an update on filming progress... but I gather plans have changed?" Sou intoned.

Amidine's grin twitched angrily. "Oh, we'll be showing you our progress, all right. Not the film, but the Rising Blue Dragon's. Well? Thanks to your help, we're a force to be reckoned with. Time to show them off."

"I'm not interested," Sou said.

"I'm assuming Lloyd taking over the lead role set you into some pathetic fit. You never were exactly mature," Shouma added.

...No holds barred.

"To hell with you!" Amidine roared. He was really driven into a corner here. "I'm sick of being used! We've got all these weapons! We've got the trade routes! And I'm a famous movie star! What do I need you for?!"

He raised a hand. His minions took aim.

If he lowered his hand, Shouma and Sou would be riddled with holes.

Yet Sou never batted an eye.

"Hmm, I knew this would happen in time, but this is faster than I anticipated."

"Yep." Shouma nodded, his tone exactly like he was kicking back in a chain restaurant, chatting with friends. "We were hoping to have the demon lords plunge the world into chaos and have your evil organization try to take advantage of that only to be mercilessly demolished by Lloyd...but you got desperate way too fast. A real passion killer."

"Tch...who the hell is Lloyd anyway?!" Amidine grumbled. Clearly, these two had anticipated this turn of events—but he didn't let that get to him. "Heh-heh-heh... Well, you two never did make much sense. One less thing to worry about! You'll die here, at the hands of my trump card. I left her alive to make Sardin do my bidding...but her daughter will fill that function just as well. She'll be here soon. Poor thing—she's no longer human."

Muttering to himself, Amidine glanced toward the sewer depths.

Sou, Shouma, and his minions all followed his gaze...

"Ooo...ooo...ooo...ooo......"

A hair-raising wail emerged from the darkness, sounding like a harmonica made of human throats.

The minions let out a series of small shrieks, and then...

Rows of humanoid faces appeared, constructed from dirt and sand, a pale blond woman—Ubi—at the center.

"Augh! Stay away!" One of the minions turned and fired at them—but the face he shot swallowed him whole.

"Tch, that fool," Amidine spat. "Well, it made for a decent demonstration."

"B-Boss?"

"Mwa-ha-ha! I took what you gave me, put the kingdom's finest minds on it, and turned it into a weapon of this magnitude!" He sounded like a child bragging about a favorite toy. "You saw what happened to my man? You'll soon share his fate!"

Neither opponent seemed the least bit perturbed.

"Oh, the Legions thing? I see you're using her as your core and forcing spirits into inanimate objects! Well worth giving you the jewel, then."

"Yeah, they'll be great villains for Lloyd to foil! Hard to look dashing when you're fighting literal dirt, though."

"Who the hell is Lloyd?!" Amidine roared. "Get them! Minions! Fire! Kill these two idiots!"

There was a hail of gunfire.

A cloud of dirt went up where the pair had stood.

A voice emerged from the debris. "What now, Sou?"

"...It seems he's here. We must hide and capture his heroics with this handy camera."

"Oh, you're right! Cool, cool. The more footage we have, the better! Such a passionate twist!"

"They oughtta be in pieces... Where are they?!"

Before Amidine could locate them, another voice rang out.

"Stop right there!"

"Huh? What now?!"

Amidine and his men swung around...and found Lloyd standing in the sewer tunnels behind them.

"I, Roy Akizuki, will not allow the villainy of the Rising Blue Dragon to continue a moment longer!"

"Y-you're...but why are you here?" Amidine yelped.

Lloyd folded his arms, legs planted firmly apart. "Heh...I need not answer to villains! Come! You have the wight to wemain silent! Argh, I blew the line!"

"......Huh?"

"Oh, sorry. Argh, I can't say sorry here! Um! Let me come in again. I hope we can edit this part out..."

Convinced he'd broken character and ruined the scene, Lloyd bowed low and raced back the way he'd come.

Between the dramatic but cheesy entrance and the display of much more convincing humility, the mob was left with their mouths hanging open.

"Boss...he's back again. What now?"

"Don't ask me! He never tires of mocking us, clearly," Amidine snarled, grinding his teeth.

Completely oblivious to this, Lloyd came bounding out of the sewer depths again.

"Stop right there!"

"We're not even moving! And you said that already!"

"I, Roy Akizuki, will not allow the villainy of the Rising Blue Dragon to continue a moment longer!"

He struck the exact same pose. Amidine looked ready to explode.

"You did this already! It's the exact same thing!" he shrieked, a vein on his forehead throbbing.

"Er, oh, sorry—let me try a different one!" Lloyd assumed he'd flubbed the take and tried to run off set again.

"No, no, no, no! Where are you *going*?! Oh, there's more of them..."

Sardin, Mena, and the Azami military forces caught up with Lloyd.

"Hey, Amidine!" Sardin growled. "It's all out in the open now. You're gonna answer for your crimes!"

Amidine just looked relieved that somebody sensible had arrived. Despite being caught red-handed, he cried out happily, "You finally figured it out, Dumb Dandy? And arrived just in time to die at—!"

"Sorry, Director, I blew a line; then he didn't like my second entrance. I'd like to start over from the top, but...can you tell me where the cameras are? I want to make sure I'm not flashing too much of my butt."

Amidine was left flapping his lips uselessly.

"Er, um. You were fine! We can edit around it. Don't, uh...worry about the cameras," Sardin stammered. He clearly decided explaining wasn't worth the effort.

Lloyd nodded gravely and bowed his head again.

"Sorry I keep causing trouble! I get it, you're deliberately hiding the cameras to elicit a more natural performance! Of course that's not what I should be thinking about. Give my apologies to the editor later."

"S-sure," Sardin replied, not sure what else to do.

As this was going on, Mena and Phyllo caught sight of Ubi's current condition.

"M-Mom!"

".........! ...This *is* necromancy."

The countless faces made from grime and dirt shocked everybody.

"That's...even worse than the stuff Rol was using." Choline shuddered.

"Gross," Riho snapped.

"Wow, even the producer is covered with mud and joining the scene! I've gotta match her enthusiasm!" Lloyd said, ever the odd man out.

Micona looked Ubi over carefully. "They're using this Ubi woman as a core to maintain the spectral faces. In my experience, we'll have to target her to resolve this."

"And there's this crowd of ruffians wielding strange guns... This won't be easy."

"Ha, never thought I'd hear defeatist talk from you, Belt Princess! Remember, you're a gaffer now! Between us and Lloyd, this'll be over in no time!"

"I completely agree with the Sir Lloyd part, but I never consented to joining your gaffing squad." Selen gave Allan and his bounce board a glare.

"Whatever," Riho said. "We've just gotta get rid of them and their dirty ghouls and get the Quinone sisters' mom to safety! Lloyd!" She shot a thumbs-up at him. "This is the action scene you've been waiting for! Show 'em what you can do!"

"Er, I can just improvise the whole thing? Director?"

"Go ahead! I'll take responsibility! Just...save Ubi!"

With Sardin's permission, Lloyd looked ready to go.

"All right! Rising Blue Dragon! These sewers will be your graves! Come on, guys! Let's save Ubi!"

And with that, the crowd of Azami soldiers surged forward, assaulting the mob.

"Come on and try us! Men! Kill them all! Or I'll feed you to the ghouls!"

That sounded like a serious threat. The mobsters quickly raised their guns.

Before they could pull the triggers...wind erupted from Lloyd's hand.

"Aero!"

The gust was strong enough to change the atmospheric pressure in this confined space. Half the firing squad was sent flying.

"Huh? Wahhhh!" Amidine shrieked, seeing his minions tumbling away. Before he'd even finished shouting, another batch of underlings was assaulted by tree roots, and he let out another shriek.

"Come on, second-years! We can't let Lloyd Belladonna hog all the limelight!"

Micona had clearly achieved full control over the treant power within her. Much like Selen, this stalker sure was willing to give up on being human.

With the treant roots taking the mobsters out of commission, Micona boasted, "Ha! They never stood a chance before the righteous might of the Azami army!"

"Micona, maybe don't claim to be righteous when using the power of a demon lord. It's hard to tell which of you is the real monster here..."

Even as Selen spoke, she was busy strangling several minions with her cursed belt.

...Which didn't, in fact, make her any better.

Riho was too busy to yell at either of them. She was using her mithril arm to knock aside the ghouls surrounding Ubi.

"Mena! Phyllo!" she yelled. "We're taking out the mobsters and the ghouls first! Then you two grab Ubi!"

"Got it!"

"Mm!"

Working in perfect sync, they started tearing through the dirt ghouls.

A few minutes later—well, faced with the combined might of the Azami forces, neither ghouls nor the mafia ever stood a chance.

"Yeesh, remind me never to go to war with Azami... Right, Amidine?" Sardin said with a confident grin.

Amidine remained sullenly silent.

"It's all over, Amidine. Give me back my wife and surrender."

"Over? How? Nothing's over! You're an ignorant fool, Sardin. This is where necromancy begins!"

With a diabolical, teeth-baring grin, Amidine pulled an ominous jewel from his pocket and began performing some sort of rite with it. A moment later, the fallen mobsters staggered to their feet, eyes hollow. The scattered piles of dirt re-formed, becoming hideous faces once more.

"Wha?"

"Surprised? Of course you are! I wiped the slate clean! This is the power of necromancy! The real ace up my sleeve!"

The jewel in Amidine's hand gleamed with a sinister light, and Ubi writhed in agony.

"Gah...guhh..."

The dirt devils, grim ghouls, and mafia mobsters clustered around Ubi, merging into one giant form.

"What is this gross thing?"

"Shocking, yes? This is the true power of the Jewel of Legions! Countless spirits melded into one hideous creature! Not something anyone can easily best!"

"...Hahh!"

Phyllo kicked it as hard as she could, sending several clods of clay and a few minions flying, but they were soon back in place. Some of the men were still conscious, possessed by spirits. Those she kicked wailed, "It hurts, it hurts!" and dug themselves deeper inside the mass.

"I can blow them all away with my spell!" Lloyd said, raising a hand.

"Don't, Lloyd!" Choline yelped. "With your power, you'll hurt Ubi, too!"

"I—I will?"

Even as they spoke, the ghoul golem was on the move, swallowing Azami soldiers in its path.

"Ack! Colonel Choline! We need a plan!" Micona called, dragging companions to safety with her roots.

Choline ran over everything Rol had told her about her necromancy research, trying to think of something.

"Right, sunlight! Rol was all smug about it! Said the spirits lose power if you bathe them in sunlight...but..."

They were in the sewers. Magic stones provided light, but that definitely didn't count.

"Too bad! Maybe if you opened a hole in the ceiling? But there's no way you ever could! The dirt monster will swallow you all! Prepare to die, Azami soldiers!"

Amidine grinned, confident their plan was impossible—without realizing he'd just given them the hint they needed.

Choline shot him a huge grin. "Aha!" she exclaimed. "Great idea! We'll go with that! Lloyd, bust a hole in the roof!"

Lloyd nodded like this made perfect sense. "Oh! That would be a dramatic scene! You've got it!"

"Huh?" Amidine gaped at him.

Lloyd rocketed toward the ceiling.

"Hup!" he yelled and kicked the ceiling as hard as he could. A very loud thud rocked the sewers.

A moment later, cracks appeared in the ceiling—and light poured through.

"All right! Micona, use your roots to keep the entire roof from caving in!"

Micona set her roots to shoring up the rafters…and the collapse was curtailed. They'd managed to avoid being buried alive, at least.

"Are you a total idiot?! You almost killed all of us!" Riho screamed.

"Settle down," Choline said. "We got the sunlight, right? Not the brightest, but…"

The ghoul golem was visibly recoiling from the light, terrified. Amidine was clearly rattled by this.

"Tch…but…a little sunlight won't be enough! It can just move to the back! I still have the advantage!

Amidine held the Jewel of Legions aloft, moving the beast.

"Bounce board brigade! V-Formation!"

At Allan's cry, his team formed ranks, redirecting the light and focusing it all on the ghoul golem.

"Wh-what?! Bounce boards?!"

Allan grinned. Their reflective boards kept the undead legions bathed in sunlight.

"Our boards are more than enough to handle this light! Keep it in the sun! We! We are the light!"

""""Yes! Lights!"""""

Whatever Allan's weirdo goals were, his brigade's efforts were knocking layers off the legions like they were applying peeling gel. Sheets of minions and chunks of dirt fell away.

And the ghouls within dissipated, banished by the light. Ubi alone remained. As the designated core, she continued to struggle in evident pain.

"Gahh…ahhh!" Ubi thrashed, possessed by a spirit, covered in mud. Azami soldiers were trying to pin her down, but she was too strong for them, and no one could stop her rampage.

""Mom!"" Mena and Phyllo were on top of her, trying to restrain her.

"Gah!" Ubi roared, trying to shake them off.

"Snap out of it, Mom! It's not like you to let some dumb ghost get the better of you!"

"……Mom! I made friends! I'm going to school! You should come see! But you have to wake up first!"

"Ga……ah…"

Ubi's struggles grew weaker.

"Ubi! Phyllo's a little dumb sometimes, but she's a good friend!" Selen cried out.

"Yep!" Riho added. "Her grades suck, but she shows up to every class!"

Subduing the mob minions, the soldiers started calling out, trying to help.

Scared the effects of the jewel were weakening, Amidine pulled a gun out of his pocket.

"Tch! She's really trying to escape the power of the jewel? You're supposed to be a zombie!"

He pointed the barrel at Mena. He'd already forgotten his plans to make use of her.

"Can't have you getting through to her—die!"

Furious that things weren't going his way, Amidine tried to pull the trigger…but Sardin saw him just in time.

"Not today!" he roared, throwing himself on top of Amidine.

"Tch! Dammit, out of my way!"

Bam!

There was a muffled gunshot.

Red bloomed from Sardin's back. Blood began to flow.

Bam! Bam! Bam!

Three more gunshots.

Sardin's coat was turning crimson, but he refused to let go of Amidine.

"Dammit! Let go! Out of my way! Everyone, out of my way! You're the king! You were handed everything in life at birth!"

"Was I?" Sardin asked, choking on the blood in his mouth. He fixed a powerful glare on Amidine. "Hardly. I could never tell the public about the wife I loved. Could never even tell my beloved daughters I was their father! There's nothing good about being king! While you…"

Sardin summoned his strength, pushing Amidine backward and swinging his fists.

"You're trying to take them from me! My wife! My daughters! My family!"

The strength of his blows sent Amidine reeling.

"Gahhhh!"

Sardin swung again, striking Amidine's chin with the full force of his emotions. Amidine toppled backward, hitting his head hard on the ground…and knocking himself out.

Clutching his belly, Sardin turned toward the Quinones.

"Ubi…," he gasped.

At this call, the light came back to her eyes.

"Dar…ling…"

The spirit possessing her finally left her body, dissipating.

Seeing her free, Mena and Phyllo moved to catch Sardin.

"…Dad?"

"Uh, ha-ha-ha, yeah, your father is King Sardin," he admitted awkwardly.

"What?! Why did nobody tell us?! All this time?!"

"Sorry…you were born in the middle of a huge fight over the succession. I'd hired your mother as a bodyguard and fell in love with her, but…"

Ubi dragged herself forward, reunited with her family.

"Mena, Phyllo, don't blame him. He hid our existence to keep us safe, to keep us out of the battle for the throne. It was supposed to be temporary, until his government settled down and things cooled off… but then I got caught."

Sardin's hand brushed her cheek. "I got you mixed up in it anyway… Sorry it took me so long."

Heedless of the blood on his hand, Ubi clutched it to her, cradling it.

Choline was already at his side, trying to heal him with her magic.

"…Crap," she said.

Even for an expert healer like Choline, the damage was too great.

Everyone could tell the wound was fatal. It was a miracle he remained conscious and talking.

Ubi stared lovingly into Sardin's eyes.

"I can finally call you my husband. At long last."

Sardin nodded wordlessly. Ubi reached out and put her arms around Mena and Phyllo.

"Sorry it took us so long—but at last we can be a family."

"……I'm sorry," Sardin whispered, well aware he was not long for this world.

Ubi shook her head, tears welling up in her eyes.

"Doesn't matter. Even if it's only for a minute—for a single second. We got to be a family. That's all the happiness I ever needed. I'll never forget this moment."

Ubi pushed Mena and Phyllo up against Sardin.

They tensed at first, but feeling their father's warmth against them—and feeling it slowly ebb away—they called out to him.

"Dad!"

"…Dad."

They found themselves crying like children.

"Oh…," he whispered. "How I've longed to hear you call me that. How I've waited for this day."

His hand reached up and stroked both his daughters' heads.

Slowly. Gently.

He stroked until no feeling was left in his fingers.

Until no strength was left in his arms.

He burned the faces of his wife and children into his fading eyesight.

Then his eyes closed, as if to sleep.

"Dad!"

"Dad!"

Mena and Phyllo clutched him tight. Tears forming in her eyes, Ubi stood, rooted to the spot.

The crowd watched Sardin's last moments in wordless silence, touched by this emotional scene.

That was the point Sou and Shouma showed up.

"Pardon the intrusion, but we're in a bit of a rush."

"Man, did we get some great footage! Yo, Lloyd! And everyone else! Super passionate performance! Bye!"

Alka was right on their heels.

"Come back here! Sou! Shouma! Whoa, is this dude dying? Whoopsie-daisy, lemme cast a little healing... Right, all better! I can bring anyone back as long as they ain't dead, but that sure was cutting it close! Mm? And this pale beauty here's got a death curse on her! Ha! This caused by that jewel Eug made, is it? Right, lemme take a look—oh, perfect! You're all better, too! Even with my powers unstable, I can handle little problems just fine. I wouldn't be myself otherwise! Bow down before my skills! I'm the greatest! Yikes, I forgot I was chasing those two villains! Later, Lloyd! Catch this kiss! Come back here!"

Having totally destroyed the mood, the three of them vanished down the sewer, leaving a stunned crowd in their wake.

Everyone had been sure Sardin was dead, but now his eyes—and jaw—opened wide.

"Huh? I'm not dead? Or even in pain? But how?"

Mena and Phyllo flung their arms around him, crying "Dad!" in much happier tones.

Ubi—now much less pale—couldn't hold back any longer. Tears flowing, she joined the group hug.

Lloyd smiled at them happily.

"I knew that was all scripted! But, man, their acting is so convincing! I really thought he was bleeding out! Pros really know their stuff! Phyllo, you got a really juicy part... Oh, and sorry. The chief and Shouma kinda burst in there—thank goodness they waited until the scene was over!"

Lloyd's obliviousness left the crowd stunned for a very different reason.

* * *

At any rate, everything had ended well...but just as everyone reached that conclusion, Amidine recovered from Sardin's knockout punch.

"Mwa-ha-ha-ha! That sure hurt, Sardin! How dare you raise a hand to me?"

"Amidine, it's all over. Give up and atone for your sins."

"Over?! Don't make me laugh! You mean to catch me? You can't! After all..."

Amidine pulled the Saint's Pendant out of his pocket, flashing a toothy grin.

The pendant's supposed ability to banish the dead was a lie, and even if it could do that, it was now nothing but a useless item handcrafted by the kid grandma.

"I still have the pendant! Without this, you can never free your wife! Ubi will be a corpse forever!"

"...Er, about that?"

It was hard to explain that a strange child—who was actually well over a hundred—had already freed Ubi from the curse while also healing a nearly dead man back to full health.

Unaware that everything had already been resolved and he was the odd man out at a happy ending, Amidine was busy acting like a triumphant villain.

Everyone but Lloyd was just giving him cold, dead stares, but he pressed on regardless, demanding, "Let me off the hook! Do that, and I'll give you the pendant! Well? Not a bad bargain, is it?"

It wasn't much of a bargain at all, since the pendant's value had long since cratered. His failure to realize that went beyond comical into outright pitiable.

But he just kept crowing. "Heh-heh-heh...go on! Nod, or I'll throw this pendant down a hole in the side of the cave!"

He started waving it around like a kid, threatening to toss it.

"Oh," Marie said, finally connecting the dots. "That pendant...if you swing it around..."

"Mwa-ha-ha! I'm not done yet! Amidine Oxo is not so easily bested! I'm at the helm of my own life, navigating a minor storm! In no time, the wind will catch my sails, and it'll be smooth—"

"That little grandma says it causes a tornado that blows away anyone who swings it."

"Mwa-ha-ha! I can feel it! I can feel the wind—the wind blowing—a bit too hard? Wait, is this pendant causing it?! Please make it stop!"

Amidine found a tornado forming around him...and the winds lifted him up, ramming him headfirst into the ceiling.

It was such a bizarre sight, no one moved to help him.

"Welp," Riho said, breaking the silence. "I know one thing for sure—that guy was pathetic to the bitter end."

Buried to the neck in the rock above, Amidine's body twitched forlornly.

"It was *Rokujou Holiday* that made him famous," Allan commented. "He played a prince who had everything you could want, but slipped out to explore the town, curious what life was like. In hindsight...perhaps a role he identified with. Some men will never be satisfied, no matter how much power they have."

As Amidine swayed, the Jewel of Legions slipped from his pocket.

It hit the ground below and shattered—as if symbolizing the destruction of Amidine's heart itself.

The next day, there was a party in the Rokujou palace garden.

At a glance, it appeared to be a wrap party for the movie, but...that film was slated to be shelved indefinitely, what with Amidine getting arrested and everything.

That fact was being kept hidden, both to avoid confusing the masses and to ensure they had identified everyone the Rising Blue Dragon was involved with.

That wasn't the only thing being kept from the public...

"What?! I can't tell anyone about my daughters?! Do you hate Daddy now?!"

Sardin was in great health—and with his biggest problems solved, making him possibly even more hyped up than usual. He was making a dramatic display of dismay as Mena and Phyllo looked on.

"...You're kind of annoying, Dad."

A phrase that would hammer a blow into any father's heart. Daughters of the world, please reserve words like this or "you stink" for when they're really needed.

Phyllo had sent Sardin to his knees, but Mena finished him off—she was back in her usual outfit, her eyes smiley once more.

"Hearing he's our dad is just not the best news. And like, we're royalty? Please. Besides, I kinda like the life I have."

Sardin looked up in horror. They weren't going to come live with him?

As his tears flowed, his wife stepped in to comfort him.

"Ubi! Say something, dear!"

"Give it up. This is how girls their age are supposed to be."

"So heartless! You may not be a zombie anymore, but are you sure your heart's beating again?"

Then Lloyd came out of the back room—in his original teenage body, but still wearing a dashing suit and tie like the grown-up version had.

Alka was following along after him, filming him with a crystal and drooling wildly.

"Maaan, grown-up Lloyd was so sweet, but boy Lloyd in a dapper suit? Total yearbook photo vibes! Good thing I retrofitted one of those to fit him."

The kid grandma was lost in her own world, as usual.

Marie was along for the ride, looking exhausted.

"I'm the one who did all the work on that suit, but do I get any thanks? And what the heck is a yearbook? But he *is* cute."

She was drooling a bit herself. Like master, like pupil.

Lloyd and his suit went over to greet Sardin.

"Director! I heard it'll be a while before the movie screens because of all the editing."

"Uh…and you are?"

"I can't wait to finish filming!"

"…You're Lloyd, right? Why are you wearing Mr. Akizuki's clothes…? Wait…"

Realizing the boy he'd met at the hotel and Mr. Akizuki were one and the same, Sardin was very impressed with Azami's disguise department. This was clearly way beyond makeup, though.

Seeing her father's confusion, Mena let her eyes widen a bit. She scratched her head.

"If you think about it, it should have been obvious he was Lloyd… If only I figured it out, I wouldn't have—"

"……Wouldn't have *what*?"

"Er, uh, nothing, Phyllo! You know, uh…I was all giving him acting tips and showing him the ropes."

Over Sardin's shoulder, Mena could see Ubi stifling a laugh. She was turning bright red from the strain of it.

"Mom!"

"Ha-ha-ha, sorry, sorry, Natie. Phyllo, better let her off the hook here."

"……Mm." Phyllo nodded once, and Ubi reached up to brush her head.

"Aww…Ubi, I want to rub her head, too!"

"…Creep."

"I'm your dad!"

"Now, now," Mena said, recovering enough to tease her father. "If you want to rub Phyllo's head so bad, we can find you a cactus. Feels basically the same."

"……Exactly the same."

"That can't be true! It would shred my hand!"

Mena turned back to Lloyd and his friends.

"'Sup, guys! How y'all doing?"

"Oh, if it isn't the famous actress-slash-princess Mena Quinone! How's it feel to be living the dream?" Riho asked like she was a red-carpet reporter.

Mena winced. "Yeah, I'm not exactly coming to terms with it."

"Figured! I sure wouldn't!" Riho slapped her on the shoulders, acting just like she always did…which was a relief.

"I was entirely unprepared!" Selen cried, barging in. "For someone like Mena to be both a successful movie star *and* of high birth? Still, never fear! I shall treat you just as I always have. If everyone started bowing to you, it would be most disconcerting."

"Spoken like a true outcast!" Riho exclaimed. "Being the Belt Princess as a kid left you pretty sharp on these things, huh?"

Selen turned and started thumping Riho with both fists, but Mena smiled at both.

"Ha-ha-ha, you're both taking it in stride, at least. Thanks—but what the heck are they doing?"

"Marie personally made these clothes?! Unhand them, Lloyd Belladonna!"

"Y-yikes! Micona! Don't!"

Micona was trying to pull the Marie-tailored suit off Lloyd, stripping him right here in front of everyone. The other girls were all watching with great interest, nobody acting all that fast to stop her.

Only Allan went barreling in at full speed.

"Unhand him, Micona! Lloyd, I'll save you!"

"Pfft, you are a man in name alone! What use will you be?!"

"Gaffer Attack! Bounce Board Three-Point Lighting!"

Allan did not hesitate to destroy Micona's eyes with his bounce boards. Using his massive frame to deploy three of them at once—a technique good kids, bad kids, and online streamers should definitely not try at home.

"My eyes! My eeeeyes!"

"…What is he even doing with his life?"

"He's certainly not trying to be a soldier anymore. And he's probably better at this…"

Allan had spent his job points in all the wrong professions, but no one blamed him for it. As long as he was having fun. Also, they knew full well that he would inevitably live to regret it and wind up sobbing into a pillow.

"Urp...huh? How do you tie this thing again?"

Lloyd had enough buttons undone his belly button was showing, and he was struggling to fix his tie.

"Uh, Lloyd!" Mena said brightly. "How's it going?"

"Oh, Mena."

"Hmm... Good, you didn't figure it out. Thought not!" She seemed as sad as she was pleased. "Lloyd, about Mina..."

"Mina? Oh, that's weird, I don't see her anywhere." He looked around, clueless as to who Mina really was.

"She's a busy woman," Mena explained, growing slightly more forlorn. "She's probably off filming somewhere."

"Oh? Well, that's a shame." He looked genuinely disappointed.

Mena held up a hand like a reporter's microphone.

"Question for ya! Lloyd, what's your take on that dame?"

"Er... She's an enigma!"

"An...enigma?"

"Yes. I think that's what they mean when they say 'she's enchanting.' I don't have a sister myself, so I'm not sure, but I bet that's what having one would be like! I'd love to see her again."

Mena's cheeks flushed slightly.

"O-oh...," she stammered. Saying more was clearly beyond her. She turned and quickly rushed away.

Ubi found her fanning her flushed cheeks. "You sure?" she asked. "You don't want to say good-bye to him as Mina?"

"I'm sure, Mom," Mena replied. "If we met now, it would just be awkward."

She looked at Lloyd, half-lidded eyes glistening. Ubi smiled in silence.

Sensing something amiss, Choline pulled her aside.

"What you looking all happy for, Mena? You're an actress and a princess and now you wanna go falling in love, too? That's too much good for one life!"

Finding out your coworker was both an actress and a princess was certainly a soap opera–worthy twist, so Choline had elected to get drunk and go after her. Perhaps not the best choice.

"It's not all good, Choline."

"How is it not?! I can see that blissful smile! I know these things! You're in love!"

"I'm not in love. It's not that..." Mena glanced toward Lloyd again. "My type is at *least* twenty. Maybe in a few years..."

"Mm? I couldn't hear you."

"Nah, nothing. So, Choline..." Mena blushed and put a finger to her lips. "Don't you go telling that boy I'm a princess—or an actress."

She winked like a girl fresh off a brief summer fling.

"...Okaaaay. So less 'good things' than 'bittersweet memories.' What happened?"

Choline cocked her head, totally lost.

It was a lot to explain. Suppose there was a love story where two people were drawn together, unaware of each other's identity, just like in the movies... Those always ended with both sides keeping their feelings to themselves.

Afterword

The following story took place before I turned thirty.

I was busy being a healthy, productive corporate drone, running myself ragged going from home to work and back again. A shuttle run with no end in sight. Then one day I was lying in bed and found myself whispering...

"Ugh, if I could just go back in time a decade...mm?"

Then I remembered what I'd been like ten years earlier.

"I know for a fact I'll be saying the same thing ten years from now."

I could see myself, nearly forty, saying something equally futile... and started to panic.

Thirty isn't too late! I've gotta do something now! That impulse drove me to my current position, here at the bottom rung of light novelists.

At the time, I was impressed with myself. Never before had I been so certain I'd achieved real personal growth.

And now?

"Aw, crap. My deadline's almost here! I should have been done by now! If only it could be a week ago...can I go back in time? Could a completed manuscript just fall out of the sky? Or grow out of the ground? Don't care which. I'm not picky..."

I swear to you, I have grown as a person.

But, like, from negative a hundred to negative fifty. The taint of failure is seeped deep into these shoulders, permeating all the way to my hips.

Hi, I'm Toshio Satou, once more wallowing in the hot springs of failure.

Somehow, we're already at the sixth volume of *Suppose a Kid from the Last Dungeon Boonies Moved to a Starter Town*! It feels like just yesterday I was sitting in a car, repeating the title over and over, afraid I'd get it wrong at the award ceremony.

Time for apologies! To my editor, Maizou, thank you for taking time to help with my work despite your busy schedule.

And Nao Watanuki, once again, thank you for the lovely illustrations. Lloyd on the cover is far too cute. It's like a DLC costume!

Hajime Fusemachi, thank you for drawing the manga every month. I look forward to seeing manga Lloyd every time.

To everyone in editing and sales, to the designers and bookstore owners—thank you.

And to my readers: Have you been enjoying the ride?

I've been able to release this many books because of you. I keep my nose to the grindstone so that you will laugh and have a good time.

I hope we will meet again in Volume 7.